I0533645

A MAGICAL MOMENT

Barbara Cartland

Barbara Cartland Ebooks Ltd

This edition © 2020

ISBNs

9781788674362   EPUB

9781788674379   PAPERBACK

Book design by M-Y Books
m-ybooks.co.uk

THE BARBARA CARTLAND ETERNAL COLLECTION

The Barbara Cartland Eternal Collection is the unique opportunity to collect all five hundred of the timeless beautiful romantic novels written by the world's most celebrated and enduring romantic author.

Named the Eternal Collection because Barbara's inspiring stories of pure love, just the same as love itself, the books will be published on the internet at the rate of four titles per month until all five hundred are available.

The Eternal Collection, classic pure romance available worldwide for all time .

THE LATE DAME BARBARA CARTLAND

Barbara Cartland, who sadly died in May 2000 at the grand age of ninety eight, remains one of the world's most famous romantic novelists. With worldwide sales of over one billion, her outstanding 723 books have been translated into thirty six different languages, to be enjoyed by readers of romance globally.

Writing her first book 'Jigsaw' at the age of 21, Barbara became an immediate bestseller. Building upon this initial success, she wrote continuously throughout her life, producing bestsellers for an astonishing 76 years. In addition to Barbara Cartland's legion of fans in the UK and across Europe, her books have always been immensely popular in the USA. In 1976 she achieved the unprecedented feat of having books at numbers 1 & 2 in the prestigious B. Dalton Bookseller bestsellers list.

Although she is often referred to as the 'Queen of Romance', Barbara Cartland also wrote several historical biographies, six autobiographies and numerous theatrical plays as well as books on life, love, health and cookery. Becoming one of Britain's most popular media personalities and dressed in her trademark pink, Barbara spoke on radio and television about social and political issues, as well as making many public appearances.

In 1991 she became a Dame of the Order of the British Empire for her contribution to literature and her work for humanitarian and charitable causes.

Known for her glamour, style, and vitality Barbara Cartland became a legend in her own lifetime. Best remembered for her wonderful romantic novels and loved by millions of readers worldwide, her books remain treasured for their heroic heroes, plucky heroines and traditional values. But above all, it was Barbara Cartland's overriding belief in the positive power of love to help, heal and improve the quality of life for everyone that made her truly unique.

AUTHOR'S NOTE

When I visited the Castles of the Loire Valley in 1990, I had forgotten that Château Chaumont was the most perfect Fairytale Castle.

In the sunshine, it looked as if it might disappear at any moment.

Because it had been spared by the French Revolution, it is without exception the most exquisite Castle in France.

One can well believe that the work, which began in 1519, by King François I was said by his rival, Charles the Fifth, the Holy Roman Emperor, to be, 'a summary of all that human industry and belief can achieve'.

Some of the rooms like the King's Bedroom, which are furnished and unchanged, make it all the more thrilling.

The successors after François' death showed little interest in Chaumont, preferring their Royal Palace in Paris.

Louis XIII made several trips to Chaumont before leaving it and the country to his brother Gaston d'Orleans.

The Prince, we are told, enjoyed showing his daughter, the future *Grande Mademoiselle*, the tricks of the famous grand staircase whose double spirals enabled two people to go up and down at the same time without ever crossing each other's paths.

There are so many Castles to see in the Loire Valley that it is impossible to mention them all.

Chaumont gave me this story and some years ago another Castle built on the edge of the dark mysterious forest of Chinon in the Indre Valley gave me another.

I was inspired to write *The Castle Made for Love* about it, just as Perrault was inspired to write *The Tale of the Sleeping Beauty*.

The Castles of Usse and Chaumont are the two most beautiful Fairytale buildings I have ever seen.

I am sure that the other Castles one by one will become centres of romance as the years go by.

We look more eagerly than we have ever done before for the real love, which seems, for the moment lost in the obsession of the media with sex, which is not the romance for which men have fought and died for over the centuries.

CHAPTER ONE
1895

"Oh, no, Papa, you cannot mean it!" Lady Lencia Leigh exclaimed.

"You promised, you promised!" her younger sister Alice cried. "How can you change your mind now at the very last minute?"

"I am very sorry, girls," their father, the Earl of Armeron, replied, "but your stepmother has set her heart on going to Sweden and a Prince does not celebrate his seventieth birthday very often."

He tried to make it a joke, but both his daughters were looking at him reproachfully.

They were thinking that ever since he had been married for the second time, the Earl had changed.

He was no longer the fond loving father that he had been before and was now someone who seemed to them almost a stranger.

When the Earl's wife had died a year ago, he had sunk into the depths of despair from which, it seemed, no one would ever be able to arouse him.

It was his good friend, the Marquis of Salisbury, who had suggested that he should go with him for a holiday in France.

The Marquis had recently built himself a very large and impressive Villa near Nice in the South of France and he had said to the Earl that he wanted his expert advice in planning the garden.

Looking back at what had occurred, his daughters realised that it had been the first step towards a tragedy.

They had never for one moment ever imagined that their father would marry again.

He had adored their mother as they all had and the whole family had been very close and extremely happy together.

It had always been a disappointment to the Earl that he had no son and therefore no direct heir to inherit his title.

But he had been extremely proud of his eldest daughter, Lencia.

She closely resembled her mother, who had been an outstanding beauty.

So great was the resemblance that at first, after his wife's death, the Earl had been almost reluctant to look at Lencia.

She had the same fair hair, the same sparkling blue eyes and the same exquisite pink and white complexion.

But Lencia also had a kind of spiritual aura about her, which made her different from all the other girls of her age.

She was also very intelligent, but that was not at all surprising considering how clever her father was.

Besides this she had a marked personality of her own that unfortunately her stepmother, the new Countess, had noticed from the moment she first stepped into Armeron Castle.

The Earl had been away from home for six weeks and they were excitedly awaiting his return and Lencia had actually received a letter from him the day before he was due to arrive.

"A letter from Papa!" she had exclaimed when the butler brought it to her.

"I hope he has not changed his mind at the last moment," Alice said, "and intends to stay on longer in the South of France."

"Papa must realise that there is such a lot to do here," Lencia assured her.

She opened the envelope as she spoke.

Taking out her father's letter, she read a little of it before she cried out,

"It cannot be true!"

"What has happened?" Alice asked at once.

Lencia looked at the letter again before she said in a voice that did not sound at all like her own,

"Papa has – married again."

"I don't believe it!" Alice declared.

But it was true.

And when the new Countess arrived, everything was changed.

The girls had waited for her apprehensively.

When their father appeared with his new wife clinging onto his arm, it was impossible for either of them to run towards him eagerly as they had always done in the past.

Madame Flaubert was characteristic of the exotic *chic* French woman. She might almost have stepped straight out of a novelette.

She was not beautiful in any way, but good-looking and she made the most of her looks.

She was amusing and witty and almost every word she spoke seemed to have a *double entendre*.

She flattered the Earl not only in words but with her eyes, her mouth and her hands.

Lencia realised that her father was fascinated by her because she was so different from the wife he had loved and lost.

Madame Flaubert had gone to visit Nice looking for a man to escort her.

The meeting with the Earl was a dream come true.

She had always hoped to marry again, but the Frenchmen who paid her compliments and laughed at everything she said did not offer her marriage.

She saw the Earl, morose and depressed, but at the same time still a very handsome man.

A rich Englishman with an impressive title!

She felt that the gates of opportunity were opening up in front of her.

She had never in her life worked so hard at presenting herself as she did after meeting the Earl.

By shameless wheedling she managed to get herself invited by the Marquis to stay in his Villa.

Her sob story was that she had been unable to get into the hotel where she always stayed and that the noise in the hotel she had been forced to go to was intolerable and the discomfort indescribable would have appealed to any kind man's heart.

The Marquis was in fact finding the Earl somewhat heavy on the hand.

Therefore he invited Madame Flaubert and another friend who he had known for years to move from where they were staying into his Villa.

From that moment, although he was not aware of it, there was no escape for the Earl.

Madame Flaubert paid him subtle compliments until he relaxed and smiled.

And then she set herself out to amuse him until he laughed.

He could not help feeling flattered when she told him how much she loved him.

He was, in point of fact, not quite certain how he found himself being married officially at the *Mairie*.

As their religions were different, they then dispensed with the usual Marriage Service to follow in a Church.

They were nevertheless legally married.

Madame Flaubert had a new gold Wedding ring on her left hand to prove it.

The Earl was not the only person who had told her all about the beauty and importance of Armeron Castle.

The Marquis, who had stayed there often, described it as one of the finest examples of medieval building in the whole country.

The gardens, which had been created by the last Earl, were to his mind, he claimed, finer than any other garden he had ever seen.

The congratulations the new Countess of Armeron had received did not however prepare her for the first sight of her elder stepdaughter.

She had expected that both the girls would be pretty.

"How could they be anything else?" she had asked the Earl. "When you, dearest, are so handsome that I know every woman's heart turns over when she looks at you."

"You flatter me," the Earl insisted, but he was quite prepared to listen to more.

The new wife, however, had a severe shock when she had walked into the drawing room where Lencia and Alice were waiting to meet her.

They felt shy and, although they tried so hard not to admit it, somewhat hostile towards their stepmother before her arrival.

They were not waiting for them in the hall, where the Earl had expected to find them.

Instead they were standing in the beautiful room that had always seemed to be the perfect background for their beloved mother.

The blue curtains and coverings on the chairs and sofas had echoed her eyes, whilst the glittering crystal chandeliers had the same sparkle that shone in her eyes whenever she saw someone she loved.

The Earl would have walked into the room first.

But his wife put her arm in his so that they came in side-by-side.

Just for a moment there was complete silence.

"Here we are, girls," the Earl began, "and I have been so looking forward to seeing you both."

With an effort Lencia moved forward.

It was then that her stepmother drew in her breath.

This was certainly a rival who she had not expected, a girl very young and so lovely that it was impossible even for a woman not to stare at her and go on staring.

Lencia kissed her father and he kissed her back.

"We have been longing to have you home, Papa," she said.

As she spoke, she could not help looking with some surprise on her face at the woman holding tightly to his arm.

The Countess had clearly dressed herself to impress.

She was wearing a hat trimmed with ostrich feathers and their colour was echoed by the ruby earrings that dangled from her ears. There was a ruby brooch pinned to the shoulder of her black satin cape.

She was certainly elegant, but at the same time there was something theatrical about her.

Lencia knew instinctively that she was just incongruous in her mother's drawing room and indeed in The Castle itself.

"Now you must meet my daughters," the Earl was saying to his new wife.

"Yvonne, this is Lencia, who, as I have told you, should have been presented in Court last year, but will instead curtsey to Queen Victoria next month."

Neither of the women spoke and the Earl went on quickly,

"And this is Alice, who is just seventeen, but I expect she will want to join in some of the Festivities that her sister is invited to."

"They are much older than I had expected," the Countess said. "I thought, dearest, seeing how young you look, your daughters would still be in the nursery."

This was obviously the sort of flattery the Earl had listened to and found so enjoyable in Nice.

Somehow it seemed more than a little out of place at this particular moment.

"I am sure, Papa," Lencia said, "that you are longing for your tea. It is all ready for you."

She moved towards the fireplace as she spoke and the Earl and his new wife followed her.

The tea was laid out as it always had been in front of the sofa.

There was the traditional shining silver teapot and kettle and also the Queen Anne tea caddy in which the very first tea from Ceylon had been served in The Castle.

There was also an imposing display of warm scones, cucumber sandwiches, fruit cakes and iced cakes and several other dainties for which the Armeron kitchens were justly famous.

As they reached the table with its long lace-edged cloth, Lencia turned to the Countess,

"Will you pour it or would you like me to do so?"

It was a question that the Countess recognised immediately as significant.

With hardly a pause she replied,

"Of course I will do it. I know exactly how your dear handsome father likes his tea,"

She swept with a rustle of silk petticoats and a whiff of exotic perfume to sit in the centre of the sofa, facing the silver tray.

It was where their mother had always sat and it was at that moment Lencia knew how much she resented the intruder, a woman who she was certain could never take her mother's place in The Castle or anywhere else.

At the same time, as the afternoon and evening passed, she had to admit that her father was in far better spirits than when he had gone away.

He was certainly finding his new wife most amusing and entertaining.

Only when they had gone upstairs to go to bed did Alice say in a whisper,

"How could he have brought anyone like that to take Mama's place?"

"She makes him laugh," Lencia had answered. "But – "

She bit back the words that she was going to say. What was the point of fighting against the inevitable?

Their father, whom they loved and who had been so very much a part of their lives, had somehow left them.

"We have lost not only our mother but also our father," Lencia said to herself bitterly as she climbed into bed.

In the days that followed she was to think the same again and again.

The new Countess was determined not to be ignored and she intended to assert herself in what she thought was her rightful position from the moment she arrived.

She gave orders to the servants in a sharp voice, but to the Earl she was all honey and sweetness.

She flattered him not only in words but by seeming to watch over and tend him.

She would fetch his cigar case almost before he wanted it and she would pat the cushion before he sat down in the chair. She was at his side almost every moment of the day.

There was no doubt, Lencia had to admit to herself, that he seemed younger in years.

Yet she felt rather embarrassed at the blatant way that her stepmother flattered her father and flirted with him quite openly regardless of who was present in The Castle.

Alice watched them wide-eyed as if it was a performance and she was the audience.

Because to Lencia her stepmother's behaviour seemed so vulgar, whenever she could she kept away from her father and his new wife.

The girls had planned with their father, before he went to Nice, that he would take them to France before the Season in London started.

Alice had been reading about the Castles of the Loire Valley.

The Earl knew them well and had promised to take the girls to see Château Chaumont, which was the largest and the most impressive of all the Castles in that part of France.

They had both been looking forward to the trip to France wildly.

To Alice it was particularly exciting because she had just grown old enough to read some of the great love stories of the world.

One which had captured her imagination more than any other had been the story of the famous beauty Diane de Poitiers.

She was loved to distraction by King Henry II of France even though she was eighteen years older than he was.

Alice was determined to see where Diane's monogram was carved on the parapet wall of Chaumont which she had restored.

"It is the letter 'D'," she said excitedly, "surrounded by attributes of the Goddess after whom she was named."

"You shall see it all, my dearest," the Earl had said, "and I promise that you will not be disappointed. I have seen a great many French Castles and Châteaux, but of them all I think that Chaumont is the most exciting and certainly the most impressive."

He sighed.

"I wish I could have stayed there when King François enjoyed the marvellous hunting available in what was then a deserted area."

The girls were listening intently and he went on,

"He had the old Hunting Lodge razed to the ground and began the construction of this sumptuous Palace, which will thrill you as it thrilled me when I first saw it as a boy."

It was the first time that her father had seemed to be enthusiastic about anything since her mother's death.

They had therefore made him plan the date they should go and how long they should stay.

"We must see heaps of other Castles too while we are there," Alice suggested eagerly.

"I can see I shall have to read up my history," her father said, "but we will certainly see all we can. I shall expect you both to speak perfect French by the time we return."

"We will try, Papa, we really will try very hard," Alice had promised.

As Lencia knew that she would, for the next month Alice talked of very little except their intended visit to France.

She sought out in the extensive library at Armeron all the books that mentioned the Loire Valley.

She had put them ready to be packed with their luggage when they set off to Château Chaumont on what to her was a pilgrimage.

Now two weeks after the Earl had returned home he was telling them that the visit would have to be postponed.

"We will go another time," he said vaguely, "I promise you."

But Alice protested volubly.

"You know, Papa, that, once we go to London and Lencia is presented, there will be too many other engagements for us to get away. And there will be

Ascot and finally Goodwood, where you will be running your horses."

Her voice rose as she cried,

"Oh, Papa, how can you fail us now when everything was fixed and planned?"

"I am sorry, my dear," the Earl said, "but 1 promise you I will find another time when it is possible for me to leave England."

The way he spoke told Lencia only too clearly that it was unlikely that their stepmother would be willing to leave during the London Season.

She was also convinced that she would not allow her husband to go off travelling with his two daughters without her.

"That reminds me," the Earl said unexpectedly. "I am afraid, Lencia, my dearest, we will have to change the Drawing Room when you are to be presented to the Queen."

Lencia stared at him.

"Why, Papa?"

"Because, my dearest, I am sure that you will understand that I must first present your stepmother on our marriage. She thinks it would be a mistake for you to be presented at the same time."

Lencia drew in her breath.

It had been planned that she should be presented last year just before she was eighteen.

Then, when the Countess died, they had been in deep mourning.

The presenting to the Queen obviously had to be postponed until the first Drawing Room the following year, which would take place at the beginning of May.

Her father had gone to see the Lord Chamberlain and everything had been arranged.

He was opening Armeron House in Park Lane and because her mother could not present Lencia, the Earl's elder sister, who was a Lady of the Bedchamber, had volunteered to do so.

It had never occurred to Lencia for one moment that, having missed her presentation last May, she would be asked to postpone it for a second time.

She knew the procedure on those occasions quite well and said,

"But if you, Papa, can present Stepmama, why in her turn, as I know has been often done before, can she not present me?"

There was a short silence before the Earl answered,

"I did suggest that, but your stepmother says, my dear, that it makes her feel old, when she is still so young, to be chaperoning a girl of your age."

Lencia knew quite well that this was not the reason.

What her stepmother was afraid of was that she would outshine her.

Because Lencia was very unselfconscious, she thought that the idea was quite absurd, yet because she was a woman she understood.

In point of fact the new Countess had been evasive about her age and she and Alice had soon realised that it was not a subject that should be discussed.

"Very well, Papa," Lencia said, "if it must be changed, then it must."

"I am sure that there will be no difficulties," the Earl said. "The Lord Chamberlain will understand and there will be several more Drawing Rooms, the last I believe is taking place in June."

"Supposing they are all full up?" Alice asked him unexpectedly.

"I cannot believe that I shall be refused a place for my daughter," the Earl asserted.

He spoke in a manner that his children jokingly called his 'Armeron air'.

It was something that happened only occasionally because the Earl was in fact a friendly and easy-going man.

But if his pride was hurt or he was insulted in some way, then his family background, which was a very distinguished one, would come to the surface and his Armeron voice would pulverise the person who had offended him.

"It would be dreadful," Alice said, "if poor Lencia has to miss being presented at Court, just as I am very sorry for myself in not being able to see the glories of Château Chaumont."

"You will see it, of course, you will see it," the Earl said. 'It is just that your stepmother has set her heart on going to Sweden and it would be very unkind of me if I refused her."

"I expect really she wants to wear the Armeron tiara and associate with all those Princes and Princesses,"

Alice said. "And I would not suppose that she knew people like that before she married you, Papa."

It was only Alice, Lencia thought, who would put thoughts like that into actual words.

Because it was something that was undeniably true, the Earl had looked at the clock on the mantelpiece and said,

"It is time we were all getting dressed for dinner. You know I dislike having to wait for my meals."

He walked out of the room as he spoke and the two girls were left alone.

"It is not fair!" Alice raged. "Our stepmother is determined that he should not go away with us. When I was talking about the beauty of the Castles, she said, 'they are not really very interesting, most of them are empty'. Fancy her feeling like that!"

Alice's voice was very scathing.

Lencia well knew that their stepmother, as the Countess of Armeron, wanted to share in the smart Society world of London and she was not the least interested in anything that had happened in the past.

"It is no use, Alice," Lencia replied. "If we cannot go, then we cannot go. We shall just have to stay here and wait for them to come back."

"When they do, I bet that she will find some way to prevent you and me going to London with her and Papa," Alice complained.

She thought for a few moments and then went on,

"She wants him to herself and to give big dinner parties at Armeron House. She will say that I am too young to attend them and that *debutantes* and their parties are a terrible bore."

"Oh, Alice, you cannot be sure she will say that," Lencia protested.

"She most surely will, because I have heard her saying it already," Alice pointed out. "She was talking to that lady's maid of hers when I passed by the door. They were speaking in French, thinking no one would understand. But I heard Stepmama say, '*debutantes* are a bore and the people I want to meet are to be found in London. So the sooner we get there, the better'."

Lencia knew quite well what her stepmother was talking about.

There had already been some controversy about the ball that her father would give for her that had been postponed from the previous year.

The discussion, when her mother was still alive, was whether they should have the ball in London or in the country.

It had finally been decided that it would be nice for Lencia to meet girls of her own age.

They would give a large ball in London and later several smaller dances in the country.

Now Lencia guessed that those plans were to be put on one side.

Of course her stepmother was bored with *debutantes*.

She could easily understand that.

Equally she felt that she and Alice were being pushed aside by a strong and determined hand.

Soon they would find themselves moving out of their father's life altogether.

'I am exaggerating everything, of course, I am,' Lencia told herself severely.

At the same time she was honest enough to know that her stepmother disliked her and found both her and Alice an encumbrance.

She was continually talking of the things that they would do in London when her father opened the house, as he intended to do at the end of the month.

It was most unfortunate, Lencia thought now, that two or three days ago the Swedish Ambassador had called at Armeron.

A neighbour he was staying with had brought him to see The Castle because it was an outstanding architectural feature of the County and a notable beauty spot.

The new Countess had made a great fuss over the Ambassador.

In fact, when they were walking in the garden, Lencia could now remember that she took him on one side.

Ostensibly it was to show him the fountain, but they were talking earnestly in French and she had wondered then what it could be about.

She knew now that her stepmother had managed to get the Earl and herself invited to the Festivities that were to take place in Sweden on the Prince's birthday.

'She is so clever with men,' Lencia thought. 'She twists Papa round her little finger and now she has done the same with the Ambassador. She always gets her own way. It is Alice and I who are going to suffer.'

They were certainly ignored for the next few days.

The Countess was in a flutter as to what she should wear in Sweden and which of the magnificent collection of Armeron jewels she should take with her.

She had them all brought up from the safes to her bedroom and sat trying on the tiaras one after another.

There was the diamond set, the emerald set and then the sapphire set and there was the pretty turquoise and pearl set too that Lencia remembered her mother wearing and looking just like a Fairy Queen.

It was a relief when her stepmother put it to one side and sniffed,

"I don't like myself in blue."

She did, however, hesitate over the sapphires.

They were a quite amazing collection that had originally been brought to England from Brazil.

When she put them on, the Countess decided that they made her look old.

"*Non, non*," she said, waving them away. "I want to sparkle and those purple eyes would haunt me!"

Finally everything was decided.

The Earl was rather surprised at the number of trunks that they were taking with them and the vast supply of hat boxes.

But he agreed with his new wife that they must do England proud.

There were not many English going to Sweden because it was so near to the beginning of the London Season.

"That, dearest, is just why they want you," the Countess told the Earl. "And who could represent the Crown and the Union Jack better than someone who is undoubtedly the most handsome man in England today?"

Lencia glanced at her father to see if this compliment was too creamy even for him.

He accepted it with a slight smile and she told herself that her stepmother was being very clever.

"Now, look after everything while I am gone," the Earl said the night before they left. "And, of course, keep the horses well exercised."

"Of course, Papa," Lencia agreed at once.

"It will not be the same as having you with us or going to France with you," Alice said in a low little voice.

Her stepmother was not then in the room, but the Earl looked rather nervously towards the door before he admitted,

"To be honest with you, my dearest, I would much rather be going to France. But I could not disappoint your stepmother, so we all three have to make the best of it."

"Yes, of course," Lencia replied, "and don't worry about us, Papa, we will be all right."

She knew as she spoke that she was speaking for herself, as Alice was looking depressed and dismal.

Then a sudden idea came into her mind.

It was so sensational that she thought that she should just laugh it off.

But when she went to bed, she was still thinking about it.

'I am crazy! Of course we cannot do such a thing,' she told herself.

But the idea did not go away.

She found herself going over it step by step in her mind.

It was just as her father had taught her to do when they had planned something together.

*

The next morning was all excitement and noise.

Her stepmother, because she was obviously feeling nervous, was speaking sharply to the servants.

Finally they did set off with the Earl and the Countess in one carriage, the brake coming behind, carrying the mountain of luggage, the French lady's maid, and the Earl's valet.

The two girls kissed them goodbye on the steps.

As the carriage went off, they waved and their father was almost leaning right out of the window to wave to them in return.

Then, as the horses disappeared down the drive, Alice turned round and walked through the hall and into the sitting room at the far end of it.

It was where she and Lencia usually sat when they were alone.

"Well, they have gone," she said as her sister came in, "and I do hope that they enjoy themselves. What are we going to do, I would like to know."

"I can tell you. You and I are going to see Château Chaumont."

Alice stared at Lencia.

"What are you – saying?" she asked.

"We are going to Chaumont to see it for ourselves," Lencia repeated. "You know as well as I do that we shall never get there if we wait for Stepmama's approval. So we have just got to be daring and go on our own. And, if you think about it, why not?"

"Why not?" Alice repeated.

There was a lilt in her voice, but she added,

"But how can we do it alone?"

"I will tell you exactly," Lencia said again, looking over her shoulder to make sure that the door was shut. "We have to be very clever about it, because no one must know where we are going and we must be back before Papa and Stepmama return from Sweden."

"That gives us all of ten days," Alice said.

"I know," Lencia replied. "I worked it out last night. Of course we cannot go alone, just two young girls together."

"Then who can we ask to go with us?" Alice enquired.

"You will be accompanied," Lencia said slowly, "by a widowed lady of about twenty-five and her name is 'Lady Winterton'."

Alice stared at her.

"But who – ?" Then she gasped, "You cannot mean – you?"

"Yes, me," Lencia said. "I have thought it all out. I can wear Mama's clothes because, as you know, we kept them all. They will make me look much older and you will just have to be yourself."

"But surely it is impossible. How can we – ?" Alice began.

"We have to be brave and we have to be very careful not to make any mistakes," Lencia replied, "but, if I am much older than you and married, I see no reason why I should not take you to France. After all, if things become difficult or we get into trouble, we can always come home."

"I believe you, *I believe you*!" Alice cried. "Oh, Lencia, you are a genius! I do so want to see Château Chaumont!"

"I know you do," Lencia said. "I asked myself why Stepmama should spoil everything. She has made Papa happy and that is all his business. But we are definitely unhappy and we have every right to fight for ourselves."

"I will fight – I am longing to fight," Alice declared forcefully.

"Well, we will have to hurry to get everything arranged."

"What do I have to do?" Alice asked her sister.

"Help me choose and pack Mama's clothes for one thing. The housemaids can do yours, but they must not see what I am doing for otherwise they will talk."

Alice nodded.

"I will not need many clothes, as we will not be staying long," Lencia went on. "But they must make me look older. I shall have to use powder and very little rouge as Mama did when she went to London."

"Mama did not use it in the daytime," Alice remarked.

"No, but Stepmama does," Lencia answered. "She is 'made up to the nines' but everyone seems to take it as normal. So I imagine that is how all the French women behave."

"Yes, of course they do," Alice said. "I have read about them and Papa told me once that in Paris the ladies look like actresses."

"Then that is how I must look as soon as we can get away from here," Lencia said. "You must tell the maids that we are going to stay with friends in London, so we will have to get ourselves taken there without anyone from the stables knowing that we are going abroad."

"That is not going to be easy," Alice commented.

"I have thought it all out," Lencia said. "We will get our own horses to take us as far as *The Three Kings*."

"Where is that?" Alice asked.

"It is a Posting inn where I know that Papa changes horses when he is driving to London. If you remember, we changed horses there the last time we went to stay with Uncle Tyson."

"Yes, of course," Alice nodded, "I remember now."

"I think," Lencia said, "we can cover our tracks better if we drive to London rather than go by train."

Alice said nothing and Lencia went on,

"It is still early in the morning so we have all day to make our plans. After spending the night at *The Three Kings*, we will hire a carriage to take us on to London. From there we can catch a train to Dover and cross the Channel on the later ferry. That will enable us to take the evening Express to Paris."

"How do you know all this?" Alice asked.

"I was working it out for our own trip with Papa before he went to stay in Nice."

She gave a sigh.

"Oh, dear, if only he had not gone. But it seemed such a good idea at the time for him to go away from everything and try to cheer himself up."

"I know," Alice said, "but we did not know that would mean *Stepmama*."

Lencia was about to say something and then thought that it would be a mistake.

Instead she said,

"Let's get on with our own plans. We just have to go over them again and again until we are quite certain that they are fool proof. Nothing – I mean nothing – Alice, must go wrong."

CHAPTER TWO

After luncheon when they knew that the servants would be busy or resting at the back of The Castle, Lencia and Alice went upstairs.

Their mother's room had been closed and locked ever since she had died. In fact the Earl had refused to have anything in her room touched or removed.

When Lencia opened the door, she was immediately vividly aware of her mother.

There was still the soft fragrance of white violets that she had always used as a perfume.

It was with difficulty that she did not look towards the bed to see if her mother was lying back against the pillows and, at the same time, holding out her arms towards her.

Lencia drew back the curtains and the bright sunshine flooded in.

She felt as if at any moment she would hear her mother speak to her and that everything would be exactly as it had been a year ago.

When her had mother died, Lencia had asked over and over again in her prayers why it had to happen.

'Why did You take her away, God,' she pleaded, 'when we needed her so desperately?'

She felt as if in some way she had been cheated out of the most important part of her life and it was difficult not to hate her stepmother even more than she did already.

But as she had said to Alice, she knew that it was no use fighting against the inevitable.

She had forced herself to remember that nothing would ever bring her mother back and that life had to go on.

No matter how difficult it would be, her father must not suffer again as he had suffered already.

As it all turned over and over in her mind, it just prevented her from crying, although she wanted her mother so much.

Everything in the room told her all too clearly what she had lost.

Then she remembered that the reason she had come to her mother's bedroom was to help Alice. It was wrong that Alice should be made so unhappy at not being able to go to France as had been already so meticulously planned.

Ever since her mother's death, Lencia had been vividly conscious that Alice had come to her for guidance and help.

Because she was the younger of the two, it was in many ways sadder for her to lose her mother and Lencia had felt that she had to take her mother's place as far as she could.

'It will make her so happy if we go to France,' she told herself, 'and whatever Stepmama may do or say, that is where we are going.'

Resolutely, but it required quite an effort, she opened up a wardrobe.

It was filled with her mother's beautiful day dresses and there was another wardrobe in the room next door, which contained all the gowns that the Countess had worn in the evening.

Alice had not spoken a word since they had come into the bedroom.

She had just stood gazing at the many photographs on her mother's dressing table, at the miniatures that had been painted when they were children and the large impressive portrait of the Earl.

This hung over the mantelpiece and was her mother's favourite.

Now, when Alice could see the long row of gowns make a kaleidoscope of colour in the sunshine, she came nearer to her sister.

"Are you really going to wear Mama's gowns?" she asked. "Papa said that no one was to touch them."

"I am going to wear them," Lencia said, "because if I am to chaperone you, I must look old enough and competent to do so."

She spoke fiercely as if she was fighting someone who was criticising her.

"Now let's choose those that will make me seem a respectable widow who would protect you if you were in any trouble."

"What sort of trouble?" Alice asked interestedly.

"We will find that out soon enough," Lencia said, "but I must be prepared to cope with it. Not as a boring *debutante* but as a lady getting on in years."

They both laughed.

Lencia lifted down from the wardrobe a very pretty gown which was in a deep blue with a little jacket to match it.

"What about this?" she asked.

"It looks rather heavy," Alice replied, "especially if the weather is going to be hot as I expect it will be in France."

Lencia thought that Alice had made a good point and so went ahead and chose another gown. It was in a paler blue and the skirt was decorated with frills, which were also repeated on the jacket.

"I remember Mama wearing this when she was going to London," she declared.

"I think it is very pretty," Alice said. "But you will want more than one."

They went through the wardrobe very carefully.

Finally they chose three smart dresses, which were all suitable, Lencia felt, for an older woman.

They then had to find the correct hats to go with them.

Fortunately those were next door in what their mother had called her 'cupboard room.'

"Now the evening gowns," Lencia said, "and, as we shall be staying in a hotel, they must not be too grand or too *décolleté*."

They chose two gowns that their mother had worn when dining at home with the family or with just two or three visitors staying in the house.

Lencia thought that she had now finished when Alice said,

"There is a gown that you would look really lovely in! You must take it."

She pointed to one of turquoise blue chiffon embroidered at the neck and round the edge of the frilly skirt with diamanté.

Lencia remembered how it had glittered when her mother wore it.

"I should have no use for that one," she said. "Remember we are going to France just as tourists."

"We might be asked to dinner in one of the Châteaux," Alice added a little wistfully.

"That is very unlikely, as few of them are lived in," Lencia replied.

"Well, bring it just in case," Alice pleaded. "You will look as pretty in it as Mama did and even if you don't ever put it on, it will at least have enjoyed the trip abroad, as I shall."

Because it pleased Alice, Lencia put it with her other clothes.

She reckoned that they would be staying for four or five days.

So she added one more simple evening gown and another day dress to her collection.

They packed them into a trunk that was fortunately available in the wardrobe room and filled two hat boxes.

"We will leave them here until the last moment," Lencia said. "Then we will put them in the corridor outside my room for the footmen to take downstairs. They will not realise that they have come from this room and not mine."

Alice agreed that this was indeed sensible.

Lencia had already told her maid that on this occasion she particularly wished to pack for herself.

She then went to her mother's dressing table to find what she knew was essential if she was to appear to be at least six or seven years older than she actually was.

She found what she was seeking at the very back of one of the drawers.

It was a little box that contained a pale but pretty shade of rouge and a salve for the lips.

She remembered her mother saying that all married women in London used powder and rouge.

"Although I don't need it," she added, "I have no wish to look like a country bumpkin."

"Do you think that will make you look older?" Alice asked.

"I hope so," Lencia replied.

She found a box of powder and a powder puff in the same drawer.

There was also a little dark pencil, which she thought her mother must have used on her eyebrows.

She put them into the trunk with her other clothes and then looked round the bedroom to make sure that they had left everything as tidy as when they came in.

Alice went out first and ran to her own room to see if the maid had packed all the gowns she had told her to pack that morning.

Lencia was alone in her mother's bedroom.

She stood for a moment, looking down at the bed where she had last seen her mother.

'Perhaps this is all wrong, Mama,' she whispered, 'without telling Papa. But it means so much to Alice to go to France. She has been very brave since you left us and needs a holiday away from The Castle. So please don't be angry with me.'

As she finished speaking, she felt as if her mother was near her and a hand was touching her forehead.

It was, she told herself, just a fantasy, but at the same time it seemed so very real and a fear came into her eyes.

'We will not do anything, Mama, that you would disapprove of,' she said softly, 'but we cannot just sit around here feeling miserable because Papa has gone to Sweden and no one is interested in us.'

Again she thought that her mother understood all that she was saying.

Then, because she was afraid of bursting into tears, she went from the room, shutting the door and locking it firmly behind her.

Now everything had been packed.

Even a number of books that Alice had collected so carefully from the library had been included in her trunk.

It was then that Lencia remembered that they would need money.

She was so used to travelling with her father, who saw to everything, including personal tips, that it had not occurred to her until then that she would have to pay all the costs of their journey.

"*Money!*" she cried to her sister. "We have forgotten money!"

"I did think about it," Alice replied, "but I thought you must have lots."

"I have very little left from my pocket money," Lencia explained, "and I expect you have spent all of yours."

"I have about two pounds in my reticule," Alice answered.

"Well, that certainly will not take us to France," Lencia said, "so we must think quickly."

Then she gave a little cry.

"I know! I know just what I must do, but we have to be careful to put it all back before Papa discovers what I have done."

"What are you going to do?" Alice asked her.

"Papa has often asked me to open the safe for him in his bedroom where he always keeps his money when he is at home. I think we shall have to raid it."

She gave a little frightened cry.

"Unless he is to find out what we have done," she continued, "which I am certain would make him very angry, we must put back every penny we take."

"I expect we shall be able to do that," Alice said. "After all we can get some money from Mr. Bentley if we give him a convincing reason for needing it."

Mr. Bentley was the Earl's secretary, who paid the wages of the household.

He also provided the girls with any cash they needed to go shopping or to buy presents.

"I can ask him for a little money today," Lencia said reflectively. "He will know we are going away, but he has to think that we are just staying with friends in London as the other servants have been told."

"Of course," Alice agreed. "But we will need a great deal more than that, enough for tips for the staff and a present for our imaginary hostess."

They both knew that this was true.

There was nothing, in fact, that Lencia could do but rob her father's safe.

She thought that she had been very stupid not to calculate from the very beginning what the whole journey would likely cost.

But she had never had to trouble her mind about it in the past. The tickets and everything else had appeared like magic when they reached the Railway Station.

It was therefore not surprising that it had not occurred to her before.

The curtains were drawn in her father's bedroom and they had to pull them back so as to see their way to the safe.

Now Lencia definitely felt that she was doing something wrong.

But then there was nothing else that she could do except give up the whole idea of going to France.

She was practical enough to realise that it would be disastrous if they ran out of money and had to apply humbly to the British Embassy for assistance.

It would be very embarrassing.

What was more, they would have to explain why their passports were in one name and they were travelling under another.

Their father had obtained for them their own passports when they had planned to go with him to France.

Before that they had been included on his, but he had said,

"You are both old enough now to have your own passports and I think you should look after them and be careful not to lose them."

Lencia and Alice had been delighted when they had seen their passports signed by the Secretary of State for Foreign Affairs.

She knelt down by the safe, which was let into the wall and hidden by a small oak table in front of it.

The Earl's bedroom was most definitely one of the show rooms of The Castle.

The huge red velvet bed had been there for generations and was ornamented at the back with the Coat of Arms of the Earls of Armeron in full colour.

Much of the furniture had also been there for hundreds of years.

The pictures on the wall were portraits of the Earls of Armeron starting with the first Earl in the armour he had worn when serving with King Richard Coeur-de-Lion on a Crusade.

As she operated the code numbers of the combination lock and then opened up the safe door, Lencia had the feeling that her ancestors were looking down on her disapprovingly.

She almost felt as if they wanted to prevent her from taking the money that she needed so urgently.

To her delight she found that there was more money in the safe than she had expected.

At the last moment she had been afraid that her father would have taken it all with him to Sweden to spend on his new wife.

But there was a large number of ten pound and twenty pound notes and a considerable pile of gold coins.

"I think we should take at least one hundred pounds with us," Alice said in a whisper.

Lencia thought that she was whispering because, like her, she thought that their ancestors were watching them.

"Surely we shall want more than that," Lencia replied.

As it was she had really no idea what everything would cost on the sort of trip that they were planning.

She took out two hundred and fifty pounds in notes and about twenty gold sovereigns.

Next she closed the safe and put back the table in front of it and then left the bedroom as quickly as she possibly could.

She felt, as she walked down the passage, that the Earls in their frames were all shaking their heads at what they considered extremely unladylike behaviour.

"Now have we forgotten anything else?" she asked Alice as they reached her bedroom.

"I hope not," Alice said. "I would have liked to take more books with me, but there was not enough room in the trunks."

"You can read them when you come back," Lencia said, "and don't forget that we have to pay back every penny we have taken from the safe before Papa opens it."

When she went to bed, Lencia went over everything again in her mind to make quite sure that she had forgotten nothing.

In fact she could not sleep because she was feeling so anxious.

She had made all the arrangements for the following morning and she had told the Head Groom that he was to drive them to where they were going to stay with friends.

The carriage with her father's fastest and best horses was waiting for them after an early breakfast at seven-thirty.

She and Alice had pulled the boxes out from her mother's room the last thing before they went to bed.

No one asked them where they were going for the simple reason that there was no one of any authority in The Castle at that moment.

Alice's Governess, who would certainly have been curious, had gone on her holidays and she would not be returning until just before the Earl and the Countess were coming back from Sweden.

'We are fortunate to have got away without telling too many lies,' Lencia said to herself.

But she knew that, after their night spent in *The Three Kings*, she would be telling what she would feel was a lie with almost every word she spoke.

At the same time she was well aware of how excited her sister was.

"We are off, we really are off!" Alice whispered as they went down the drive.

The way she spoke told Lencia at once that she had been frightened up to the very last minute that something might turn up to stop them.

Instead they were on their way, travelling very fast in the light chaise that their father had specially built for long journeys.

The London road was a good one and well paved.

They reached *The Three Kings* quite easily by teatime, having stopped for nearly an hour for luncheon.

Lencia had explained to the Head Groom, who was driving them, that their friends were picking them up at the inn.

If he took the horses back slowly, they would not be overtired.

"You leave it to me, my Lady," the Head Groom replied. "I'll not run them off their feet, you can be sure of that."

"Of course I can,'" Lencia said, "and thank you so much for driving us so comfortably."

Alice thanked him as well and they then walked together into *The Three Kings*.

It was a large and impressive Posting inn.

The proprietor remembered Lencia from when she had come with her father.

"'Tis a privilege and honour to see your Ladyship again," he said bowing. "Will you be stayin' with us or just havin' a break on your journey."

"My sister and I would like to stay the night," Lencia responded, "and we would also be grateful if tomorrow you could provide us with a fast carriage to take us into London."

The proprietor looked slightly surprised although he did not say anything.

He showed them into what Lencia was aware was one of their best bedrooms. Her father had occupied it the last time they had come here.

Because she thought it wise in case anyone who knew them happened to be in the inn, they had dinner in a private room although it cost more.

In fact when Lencia saw what she had to pay for their bedroom and their dinner, she was glad she had taken as much money as she had from her father's safe.

The carriage that conveyed them to the Railway Station in London was also expensive.

As her father had always done, she gave the driver a good tip.

When she came downstairs in the morning, she had hurried through her goodbyes to the proprietor.

She hoped that he would not notice how different she looked from when she had arrived.

However, as he was an elderly man and wore spectacles, she thought that he would not notice.

She had put on one of her mother's gowns and packed the one that she had arrived in and she put on a hat of her mother's and felt as if everyone would be staring at her.

She had rather cheated on her face, using only a little powder and not adding the salve to her lips.

'I will put that on later,' she told herself.

Alice, of course, noticed the difference immediately.

"You do look older," she said when they were seated in the Posting carriage. "In fact I would think you were getting on for thirty or more rather than a girl of not yet twenty."

"I hope that everyone thinks the same," Lencia said, "and I must carry myself in a very dignified way. I am just wondering if it would have been wiser if I had said that you were my daughter."

Alice laughed.

"I think that would strain their credulity. To tell you the truth, Lencia, you look very very pretty just as I remember Mama looked lovely in that hat."

"Well, remember from now on that I am 'Lady Winterton'," Lencia said, "and that your name is 'Austin'."

"'Alice Austin' does not sound too bad," Alice said, "and thank Goodness we have not changed our Christian names otherwise I would never remember."

"It is very important we don't make a mistake," Lencia told her again.

She repeated this as they finally reached the Station.

Then the luggage was taken from the carriage by a porter.

As he moved away, after asking what train they were travelling on, Lencia stopped him.

"One moment," she said. "I am afraid I forgot to put the labels on our luggage. Would you be very kind and tie them on for me please?"

She handed them to him as she spoke.

On three of them, boldly written in black ink, was 'Lady Winterton' and so on the other two, 'Miss Alice Austin.'

The porter obligingly tied them on the different trunks and hat boxes, there were three of them because Alice had one too.

Lencia tied another label onto the basket she was carrying, which contained some food for them to eat on the train.

She thought that it would be a silly mistake to go to the restaurant car.

Alice also had a hand case on which she tied a label. This she had packed herself and Lencia knew that it contained a number of books on the Castles of the Loire and especially on Château Chaumont.

Alice had talked so much about the Castles of the Loire and now that they were actually on their way to them Lencia was worried that she might be disappointed when they actually reached Chaumont.

The porter was impressed by her title and so found them a compartment marked *Ladies Only* which was empty.

"You be early, my Lady," he said. "I'll try and get the guard to lock you in in case there be a large crowd at the last moment."

"That will be very kind of you," Lencia replied.

She gave him a tip and, as he thanked her profusely, she just wondered if it had been too large.

He kept his word and the guard came and locked them in.

They were thankful that he had done so, because five minutes later what seemed to be a whole school descended onto the platform.

They were a noisy collection of teenagers and the people who were with them and the porters were having some difficulty in preventing them from invading every carriage whether it was First, Second or Third Class.

Finally they were all accommodated in Third Class carriages and then a large number of other passengers climbed onto the train as well.

"We are lucky to be on our own," Alice pointed out.

"I had never expected that there would be such a crowd," Lencia replied, "but now we can eat our luncheon in peace as soon as you feel hungry."

She herself was still too agitated and apprehensive to want to eat anything.

However the barley water that they had brought with them seemed delicious and there was also some fruit.

The train took longer than they had expected to reach Dover.

Every time they stopped, Alice was afraid that something had gone wrong and that they might not catch the late afternoon ferry to Calais.

"I am sure it will wait for the train with all these people on it," Lencia said soothingly.

"It would be no use waiting if the train had broken down and trains do break down," Alice answered. "I have read about it in the newspapers."

Lencia laughed.

"The newspapers tell you only when things go wrong and never when they go right. I am quite sure, Alice, that, as all has gone well so far, we are going to be lucky."

"I do hope so," Alice replied uncertainly.

*

They actually reached Dover punctually.

As they went aboard the ferry that was waiting for them, Alice was too happy to speak.

It was a warm day with no wind and the sea looked very calm.

They saw passengers going down in herds below deck, but Lencia had decided that she would rather sit outside for as long as it was possible.

Alice thought the same and so they found two comfortable chairs from which, as the ship sailed, they could see the White Cliffs of Dover in all their glory.

"We have done it! We have really done it!" Alice cried. "And I thought last night that something was bound to stop us at the very last moment."

"Well, your wish has come true," Lencia said, "and we cannot possibly ask for more."

"I am going to ask for a great deal more," Alice declared. "I want to see every Castle in the Loire Valley before we go home."

"That might take you years," Lencia protested, "and just think of the commotion if Papa comes home and finds us not there."

Alice laughed.

"It would serve him right for being so unkind and breaking his word to us."

"Perhaps one day we will tell him how clever we have been in going to France without him," Lencia said. "But for the moment, let us not count our chickens before they are hatched and we must make sure that we don't make any stupid mistakes."

The ferry had been under way for some time when Lencia became aware that there was a man staring at her and Alice with curiosity.

He was walking round and round the deck as a number of other men were doing and he passed them several times, but each time he drew a little nearer to where they were sitting.

Also, she thought, he moved a little more slowly.

He was certainly not English, but was possibly French.

He was dark, not particularly tall and seemed, she thought, to be about forty years old. He was dressed elegantly with a cape over his shoulders, which she knew the smartest men affected when they were travelling.

She had been aware of him for some time before Alice asked,

"Who is that man who keeps looking at us? Do you think he knows who we are?"

"I hope not," Lencia said. "I am sure I have never seen him before."

"He keeps looking and staring at us," Alice said nervously, "in a funny sort of way."

Lencia thought that it was perhaps because they were two women travelling alone.

Then, as the stranger came round for the fourth, or was it the fifth, time, he stopped.

Lifting his hat, he spoke to Lencia, saying,

"Forgive me for introducing myself, but I am the Comte de Pontlevoy and I am sure I have met your husband, Lord Winterton, on several occasions."

Lencia looked up at him, realising that she had been right in thinking that he was French.

He spoke English very well, however, with only a slight accent.

For a moment she could not think of what to say and then in a low voice she replied,

"My – husband – is dead."

"I am very sorry to hear that," the Comte replied. "I always found him a charming and very interesting man. I had no idea that he was married."

Lencia was wondering frantically how she should reply.

Then she was aware that the Comte was not looking at her but at Alice.

She was looking very pretty in a green travelling gown which was a perfect frame for her translucent skin. It also accentuated the colour of her hair, which was dark like her father's.

There was no doubt that Alice was extremely pretty.

She was only at the moment overshadowed by Lencia, who with her mother's beauty left those meeting her for the first time speechless.

Without waiting for an introduction, the Comte held out his hand to Alice.

"I am sure you are enjoying the sea voyage," he said. "Is it your first?"

"Yes, it is," Alice replied, "and I am finding it very exciting."

"It is something I always enjoy," the Comte replied. "You must tell me what are your first impressions because that is something that one never forgets."

As he spoke, he moved from standing in front of Lencia and sat down on a chair beside Alice.

As he did so, he knocked against the bag that she had put at her feet.

Lencia had done the same with hers and now she understood, almost as if it had been pointed out to her, how the Comte had managed to introduce himself.

She had put at her feet the basket which she had carried their food in.

Its label was hanging from the handle that it had been tied to and would have been easily readable by those passing by.

The Comte, if indeed he was one, had obviously wanted an excuse to start speaking to them.

She had provided it, very stupidly, she now thought.

"We are on our way to Blois," Alice was saying, "because we are going to Château Chaumont, which I have longed to see for years."

"So I shall have the pleasure of seeing you there," the Comte said, "as I live quite close to Chaumont. In fact I am returning there now after a visit to friends in England."

"Then you know The Castle well?" Alice enquired. "Is it as beautiful as it sounds?"

"Even more beautiful," he replied, "and I hope I shall have the pleasure of showing you round."

There was something in the way he spoke that made Lencia feel uneasy.

He had forced an introduction for himself, she was quite certain of that.

Now he was making arrangements to show Alice round Chaumont and so she wondered quickly what she should do.

Picking up the hamper at her feet, she said,

"I am feeling rather cold, Alice. I think we should go below. It would be a great mistake to catch a chill."

"Yes, of course," Alice replied immediately. "But this gentleman is now telling me about Chaumont."

With her head in the air and walking with what she hoped was dignity, Lencia walked away.

There was nothing that Alice could do but follow her.

"I will see you again," the Comte said as she rose to her feet. "You can be quite certain of that. We will talk about the beauty of Château Chaumont and, of course, yours."

Alice looked at him wide-eyed.

She was not quite sure that he had said the last words, but if he had, they seemed to her very strange.

"I must go after my sister," she said rapidly.

Picking up her bag of books she then hurried after Lencia.

The Comte sat, watching her go, a smile on his lips.

Alice caught up with Lencia just as she was going down into the Saloon.

"Why did you go away like that?" she asked her. "The Comte who spoke to us lives near Chaumont."

"He may or he may not," Lencia said. "He picked us up in a blatant way by pretending that he knew my husband, who you know as well as I do does not exist."

"There may be a Lord Winterton for all we know," Alice retorted.

"What I do know," Lencia replied, "is that the Comte read the name on the label I very stupidly put on this basket and thought it was a good way to make our acquaintance."

Alice stared at her in astonishment.

"Do you really think that is what he did?"

"I am quite certain of it," Lencia said, "and it would be a great mistake, dearest, for you to know men like that."

Alice said nothing.

She thought as they found a place to sit below that she would much rather have been on deck talking to the Comte about Chaumont.

But, of course, Lencia was so right and they must not talk to strange men.

After all he might be a crook looking out to steal other people's property.

She could not, however, help looking for him in the crowds when they reached Calais.

It was getting dark and the dim lights seemed to make it more difficult to see.

Just as they were getting into the Express train for Paris, Alice heard a voice behind her.

It was the Comte.

"Don't forget me. Miss Austin," he said. "We will meet at Chaumont and I will tell you all sorts of fascinating stories about it which other people are unable to do."

"Oh, thank you, thank you," Alice enthused, "I do hope you will not forget."

"You can be quite certain I shall not," the Comte replied.

Alice smiled at him.

Then, as she realised that Lencia had gone ahead of her into the train, she hurried up the steps to follow her.

They had a sleeping carriage to themselves and the beds were already made up.

"I have never slept in a train before," Alice said, "it is very new and thrilling."

"What did that man say to you?" Lencia asked in a cold voice.

"He said he would see me in Chaumont and tell me lots of things that other people could not tell me," Alice replied. "That is what I want to hear, Lencia, and it is no good being too disagreeable towards him or we shall be left just to the guides."

"I don't trust him," Lencia said. "And we have to be very very careful whom we talk to on this journey, as we have no man to protect us."

Alice did not answer, thinking that her sister was being unnecessarily prudish.

There could not be any harm in speaking to a French Comte, especially if he was talking about Château Chaumont.

CHAPTER THREE

The train arrived duly in Paris at seven o'clock the next morning.

A Steward had told Lencia that she need be in no hurry to get off the train at once, as it stayed at the same platform for nearly two hours.

But because Lencia had no wish to see the Comte again, she insisted that she and Alice leave almost as soon as the next train arrived.

She had deliberately not gone at dinnertime to the restaurant car that was attached to the train as she just knew that it would be impossible there to avoid the Comte.

She had instead asked a Steward to bring some food to their compartment and they also ate the remainder of the fruit and some homemade cake from her basket.

Alice thought that Lencia was being very fussy about the Comte, but decided it wiser to say nothing.

They found a porter to collect their luggage and a *fiacre* then took them from the *Gare du Nord* to the *Gare Montparnasse*.

Here they were lucky.

Although they were early, a train for Blois was in the Station and they found themselves a comfortable compartment.

"Now we are on the last lap of our journey," Alice said delightedly.

She opened her bag and took out a book about the Château Chaumont to read extracts from it to her sister.

"Those are all the things I want to see," she said, "and I hope that there will be someone to show me the places that are not open to the ordinary members of the public."

Lencia knew that she really meant the Comte, but thought it best not to argue over it until the occasion arose.

She was quite certain in her mind that the Comte was an undesirable acquaintance, but she knew that she had no valid reason for saying so.

'I just instinctively feel that he is unpleasant and untrustworthy,' she told herself.

She remembered how her mother had always said that she had an instinct as to whether a person was nice or nasty.

It was not what they said or did, but what they were.

They seemed to have been waiting for such a long time in the *Gare Montparnasse* before finally the train began to move.

They had not been locked in their compartment as they had been in England and two other passengers had stepped in with them at the last moment.

One was an elderly man who closed his eyes rapidly and went to sleep.

The other was a woman with a small dog which she held in her lap.

They did not, to Lencia's considerable relief, seem in any way interested in her and Alice and very quietly

Alice continued to read extracts from her book about Chaumont.

It was not a long journey.

Before they did arrive they passed through some very beautiful country and there were a few Châteaux to be seen in the distance.

Alice grew more and more excited.

"Look, Lencia," she kept saying, "there is a Château amongst the trees. I wonder if it is in my book – but I am not quite certain where we are."

Her excitement made her look even prettier than usual.

Lencia thought again that she must be careful and protect her from men like the Comte.

It was something that she had not anticipated when she had been planning their journey to France with her father.

She still thought of her sister as being quite young and still in the schoolroom.

The mere idea of there being any danger from men had never occurred to her.

Now, for the first time, she thought that maybe she would have been wiser to wait and hope that their father would take them to France when he had the time.

But she was very certain that it would have meant that Alice would have continued to be disappointed.

That did seem unfair, especially when they had spent all last year in such heavy gloom in mourning for their mother.

Alice had missed her more than anyone else did, except, of course, her father and it had not helped when they received no invitations from any of their friends, who thought that they were being tactful.

Lencia was quite sure also that people generally avoided those who were in mourning as it made them feel depressed too.

Everyone had to die sooner or later, but there was no doubt that the majority of people looked on death with horror.

It was something that they did not wish to think about until it actually happened.

When the train pulled into Blois, Alice was almost jumping for joy.

"We are here! *We are here!*" she cried. "I was so certain that something would prevent us from actually arriving."

"Well, thank Goodness, you were wrong," Lencia said. "Now let's find our luggage and try to find somewhere to stay before you rush off to see the Châteaux."

They then climbed out of the carriage and onto the platform.

The Station was not a very large one, but there was no sign of a porter.

They walked to the far end of the train and here they found one old and rather decrepit-looking porter very slowly pulling luggage out of the guard's van.

Lencia looked at it and saw that it was packed full.

There was not only passengers' luggage but also a number of large wooden crates, which looked very heavy.

In her excellent French she said to the porter,

"We have two trunks in the guard's van. Would you be kind enough to take them out?"

"I've got to move what's in front of 'em first," he answered in a surly voice.

"But that will take ages," Alice protested.

Lencia was also certain that the porter would not be strong enough to move the crates himself.

There were some smaller pieces of luggage at the side of them and passengers picked up their own baggage and walked off with it, not waiting for any help from the porter.

Too late Lencia realised that, since they had arrived at the Station in Paris so early, their luggage had been put into the back of the guard's van.

With only one elderly porter, it would be impossible to extract it for what might take a long time.

"I don't know what we can do," she murmured to Alice.

"But we must get our things out, Lencia, we must!" Alice insisted. "Shall I climb in to see if I can find them at the back?"

"No, of course not," Lencia answered. "Besides, even if you find them, you can hardly lift them out yourself."

"But we must do something," Alice moaned desperately.

It was then that a voice behind them came in perfect English,

"I wonder if I can help you, ladies?"

Lencia turned round.

Standing just behind them was an extremely handsome gentleman.

In fact he was so good-looking that she could not help staring at him in astonishment.

Then she realised that he was smartly dressed and had a noticeable air of authority about him.

"We caught the train early," she said, "and I am afraid our trunks are right at the back of the guard's van behind those crates. There does not seem anyone capable of collecting them for us."

The man talking to them looked into the guard's van and then turned round.

Behind him Lencia saw that there were two servants wearing very smart uniforms.

He spoke to them, then turned back to Lencia and said in English,

"My servants will find your luggage if you will be kind enough to tell them what they are to look for."

"Thank you very much," Lencia said gratefully.

Speaking in French she explained that there were two trunks and three hat boxes.

"They are labelled," she added, "Lady Winterton and Miss Alice Austin."

The servants moved towards the guard's van and the gentleman who had spoken to them said as they went,

"I must apologise for blocking up the van with the crates that are now being taken to my Château.

"They are certainly too heavy," Lencia replied, "for my sister and me to move."

The gentleman smiled and Alice added,

"Thank you very very much for helping us. We might have had to wait here for ages and I want to hurry and see all the wonderful Châteaux of the Loire, which is why we have come here."

The gentleman smiled again.

"It is for that reason that most people come to Blois and I do hope that you enjoy them."

"I am sure we shall," Alice said, "I have read so much about them and they all sound too fabulous to be true."

Then they all three of them stood watching the gentleman's servants as they moved one of the crates out of the guard's van and pushed another to one side to reach their luggage at the back.

While they were doing so, passengers kept coming up and taking away their belongings.

It made it easier when Lencia's trunk was found to bring it out onto the platform.

Alice's came next and then the three hat boxes.

Lencia gave a sigh of relief.

"Thank you, thank you very much," she said, "you have been very kind and we are most grateful."

One of the servants had produced a trolley as if from nowhere and lifted the luggage onto it.

"I presume," the gentleman said, "you will need a carriage. Where are you staying?"

Lencia hesitated.

Then, because he had been so kind, she said,

"I wonder if you could give me the name of a quiet and respectable hotel. As you have heard from my sister, we are here to view the Châteaux.

"I am afraid a great number of people come for the same reason," the gentleman replied. "So the few hotels that there are in this area are usually overbooked."

Lencia drew in her breath.

She had not thought, which was perhaps very foolish of her, that they should book their accommodation before they actually arrived.

Alice gave a little cry.

"But we must be near Château Chaumont," she said. "I want to spend lots and lots of time there and it may be difficult if we have to stay far away from it."

She looked up pleadingly at the gentleman.

"Please think of a hotel that is near to Chaumont."

The gentleman hesitated and then he said,

"Perhaps I should introduce myself. I am the Duc de Montrichard and, as it happens, the Guardian of Chaumont."

Alice gave a little gasp of delight and stared at him wide-eyed.

"I am afraid," he responded, "that you are going to find it extremely difficult to find any accommodation in any hotel. May I therefore invite you as my guests to my own Château, which is not very far away?"

Alice gave a cry of excitement.

But Lencia quickly said,

"We could not accept, *monsieur*, to be an encumbrance on you, although it is extremely kind of you to suggest it."

"You would not be an encumbrance," the Duc replied. "As I have only just returned from spending some time in Paris, there is, I can assure you, plenty of room in my Château to accommodate you and your sister."

"Oh, thank you, *thank you*," Alice said before Lencia could speak. "It would break my heart if I could not see Château Chaumont after coming all this way."

"Then it is something we must prevent at all costs," the Duc said with a smile. "So let's get into my carriage, which is waiting for me outside and my servants will follow with your luggage."

Without waiting for Lencia to speak, he gave instructions for the servants to carry their luggage out of the Station.

The crates were to be fetched later.

And then he walked down the platform with Lencia on one side of him and Alice on the other.

"I feel very embarrassed," Lencia said, "thrusting ourselves upon you like this."

"You are doing nothing of the sort," he said. "As I have just told you, I am not having a house party at the moment and you will find only my nephew, the Vicomte Bethune, waiting for us at Château Richard."

"It has been a dream of my sister's for years to see the Castles on the Loire," Lencia said. "We have come unexpectedly and in a hurry, which is my only excuse for not being sensible enough to book our hotel rooms before we left England."

"Well, I promise you that your sister shall see all the secret parts of Château Chaumont that are not open to the public and she could not do that without my authority."

"That is what the Comte de Pontlevoy has promised us," Alice said impulsively. "But Lencia did not believe that he was telling the truth."

"Pontlevoy!" the Duc exclaimed. "How do you know that man?"

"We do *not* know him," Lencia said quickly. "He quite blatantly picked us up on the ferry because he saw our names on the labels of our hand luggage."

"It is the sort of thing he would do," the Duc answered. "I advise you, *madame*, to have nothing to do with him."

"You are telling me exactly what I thought instinctively," Lencia said, "but my sister in her innocence proclaimed that she was very interested in Chaumont and he promised to show her all the treasures that the ordinary visitor is not permitted to see."

"Which is not in his power to do," the Duc said loftily. "Unfortunately he does live in this neighbourhood, but he is a man I should not recommend as a suitable companion for a young girl."

He glanced at Alice as he spoke.

Lencia thought that she understood exactly what he was implying.

"Then I am very grateful, *monsieur*," she said, "that you have warned us against him for I am quite certain that he intends to be a nuisance where my sister is concerned."

"He is notorious for that," the Duc said in a low voice.

Lencia drew in her breath.

She knew now that they had been through a very narrow escape.

It had been very silly of her not to realise that there were unpleasant men who would be attracted by young girls.

No one could look prettier than Alice looked at the moment.

Outside the Station there was an open carriage drawn by two extremely fine horses.

The Duc helped them into it and there was room for all three of them on the back seat.

He sat between them, saying that he would explain to Alice the Châteaux they passed on the way to his own.

"It is very very exciting for me," Alice said, "and please will you make it possible for me to see round as many Châteaux as we can before we have to go home. But then, of course, the most important and the most inspirational and the one I have dreamed about is Chaumont."

She spoke so eagerly and so excitedly and enthusiastically that Lencia thought that the Duc must be impressed by her sincerity."

"My sister," she said, "has read every book in our library about Château Chaumont."

"Where do you live?" the Duc asked suddenly.

His quite natural question took Lencia by surprise.

She had not thought that she would have to explain to anyone in France where she lived.

She certainly could not say Armeron Castle, which she was sure would be known even in France.

Thinking quickly she then replied,

"I have a house in London and also one in Kent."

"And your husband is not with you," the Duc asked.

"I am a widow," Lencia replied.

"Forgive me," he remarked, "but you seem too young to be bereaved."

Lencia thought it best not to reply to this.

She merely looked ahead and then, as they crossed a bridge, she enquired,

"Is this really the River Loire we have just crossed over?"

"It is indeed," the Duc answered.

"It looks very lovely," Lencia said, "in the sunshine."

"So will Chaumont, which you will see in a moment," the Duc replied.

They drove on and only a few minutes later they came in sight of Château Chaumont.

It was lying a little below them and at the sight of it Alice gave a cry of sheer delight,

"It is just as beautiful as I expected it to be."

The Duc ordered the carriage to come to a standstill.

As Alice stared at Château Chaumont with its four Towers, the Duc said with a smile,

"It has more than four hundred rooms, fourteen great staircases, seven minor ones and three hundred and sixty-five fireplaces."

Lencia laughed, but Alice stated seriously,

"I want to see them all, every one of them."

"I am afraid that would take a very long time," the Duc said. "But I promise that you will see not only the best of Château Chaumont but also parts that are not open to the public and for which only I have the key."

"Oh, thank you – thank you!" Alice cried. "Can we start now?"

Lencia spoke before the Duc could answer.

"No, of course not! Monsieur le Duc wishes to return to his own Château."

Alice realised that this was a rebuke.

"I am very sorry," she said. "It is all so exciting – and even more exciting now that we have met you, *monsieur*."

"That is the sort of compliment I like," the Duc replied with a twinkle in his eyes.

"But I do mean it," Alice said, "because now we shall not have to trail around with a group of sightseers and you promised that I shall see the secret places where no one else is allowed! Oh! I am so glad we came."

"So am I," the Duc added.

He was answering Alice, but he was looking at Lencia.

As she met his eyes, she suddenly felt shy.

She had the feeling that he was looking at her not exactly with admiration but in a way that seemed somehow more intimate.

Then she told herself that she was meant to be a widowed woman of a certain age.

Therefore a gentleman like the Duc would be more at home with her than he would with a young girl or a *debutante*.

She remembered her father saying to her once that when he was a young man he avoided *debutantes*. And like all his contemporaries, he was afraid that he would be married off to one of them by some ambitious Mama.

"I therefore," he had said, "spent my time with married women who were very beautiful and very amusing but who could not tie me to them with a Wedding ring."

"But you married Mama," Lencia had then pointed out.

"I fell in love with your mother the moment I first saw her," the Earl replied. "She was the most beautiful women I had ever seen in my whole life. I was determined to get to know her and, as soon as we were introduced, I knew that I was really in love."

His voice had deepened as he went on,

"And she miraculously fell in love with me. It was the great romance of the Season and, as you know, we lived happily ever after."

Lencia thought now that the Duc if he was unmarried, would, like her father, be avoiding *debutantes.*

'In which case,' she thought, 'as he supposes I am so much older, we should be able to talk to each other without any difficulty.'

She knew now why she had been aware, before he told her who he was, that there was an aura of authority and consequence about him.

Then, when she saw his Château, she could understand it even more clearly.

Château Richard was sublimely magnificent,

Even Alice, who was always so bemused by Château Chaumont, could not help thinking that it was overwhelming and at the same time out of this world.

They turned up a long drive, rising all the time, higher and higher.

They were to learn later that Château Richard had been erected on the site of a former feudal Castle that had ruled and protected the countryside which lay beneath it.

Richard had a central Pavilion in the Renaissance style and a huge Tower with a dome.

The exterior was very impressive and Lencia knew that the moment she stepped inside that the Duc lived in great luxury and his Château was also a Palace fit for a King.

They entered a great hall in which there were a number of servants on duty in the Duc's fine Livery.

Next a young man came running down the stairs.

"You are back, Uncle Valaire," he exclaimed. "Did the crates arrive safely?"

"Quite safely, Pierre," the Duc replied to him. "They are on their way here and I have brought two guests who want our help in seeing all the Châteaux of the Loire."

Pierre was, Lencia thought, a good-looking young man of around twenty-one or twenty-two.

Then he was bowing respectfully in front of her.

"This is my nephew, the Vicomte Bethune," the Duc was saying. "Pierre, this is Lady Winterton and her sister, Miss Alice Austin."

Pierre kissed Lencia's hand, as was correct, and then shook hands with Alice.

"It was very clever of my uncle to find you," he said, "as well as the crates, which have arrived from Paris after some delay."

"I do hope we are the more important," Alice said. "But we are very grateful to the crates because it was really they who introduced us to your uncle."

"That is true," the Duc nodded, "and now that we have visitors, I am quite sure that they are as hungry as I am for luncheon."

"You are so late," Pierre replied, "that I very nearly ate it all, but it is in fact waiting for you in the dining room."

The dining room was as magnificent as the rest of the Château Richard.

As they ate, the Duc told them a little about important visitors who had in the past stayed in

~66~

Château Richard and the names of those great men who had contributed to the treasures in it.

It was only a light meal and, when it was over, Alice looked at the Duc beseechingly and it was impossible for him not to understand her intent.

"I know what you are asking," he commented. "You want to go to Château Chaumont."

"Oh, please, please, if I can go just for a few minutes," Alice begged. "Having waited so long, I feel I cannot wait until tomorrow."

"Really," Lencia admonished. "I think you are asking too much of Monsieur le Duc after he has been so kind to us."

"Chaumont is fortunately only a few minutes' drive away," the Duc said, "and we will go there at once so that Alice can sleep peacefully tonight. Otherwise I am sure that she will stay awake fearing that it will vanish before the morning."

"That is exactly why I want to go there now," Alice pointed out in a low voice.

The Duc looked at Lencia.

"Will you come too, Lady Winterton?" he asked. "Or are you too tired?"

"Of course I am not too tired," Lencia laughed.

Then she remembered that she was supposed to be older and added in explanation,

"I live mostly in the country and so I can assure you that we are far more energetic there than those who live in London."

"I am quite prepared to believe you," the Duc smiled, "so we will all go to Chaumont now and if our legs ache after climbing all those staircases, we can blame your sister."

Alice laughed and Pierre chimed in,

"I will race you up them and I am quite certain that I shall win."

"And I shall make sure you don't," Alice retorted. "Like all men you think women are weak little things who faint at the idea of having to climb up a staircase. At this moment I am quite ready to climb to the top of the Tower and dance on top of it."

They laughed at this admission by Alice.

But Lencia knew that it was worth all the difficulties that they had been through to see her sister looking so happy.

It was indeed, as the Duc had said, only a short drive from his Château to Chaumont.

When they arrived there, he took them in through a door that he alone had the key for and they were now in a part of Château Chaumont where visitors were not admitted.

"I am going to show you only a very few of the most important things today," he said. "Tomorrow we will take much longer, that is, if you are still interested."

He was teasing Alice, but she parried,

"Of course I will be interested. I cannot tell you how excited I really am at being here and seeing this wonderful Château."

She put out her arms as she spoke almost as if to embrace all of Chaumont itself.

Alice had already told the Duc what she most wanted to see, so he took them first to the bedrooms of the two rival owners of Château Chaumont, Diane de Poitiers and Catherine de Medici.

He also showed them the bedroom of the Astrologer Ruggieri, an inveterate plotter and the Queen's so-called evil adviser.

There were some beautiful pieces of furniture and tapestries dating from the Renaissance period and Alice also saw the letter 'D', which Diane de Poitiers had ordered to be carved on the parapet.

She put out her hand and touched it very gently and they all knew how much it meant to her.

Then they went to view the Royal Apartments of King François I.

There was a great deal of beauty to admire there.

While Alice and Pierre were looking at something else, the Duc then showed Lencia the famous lines the King was supposed to have had engraved on a window in his study.

"*Woman is fickle. Mad is he who relies on her.*"

Lencia read it and then she enquired,

"Is that what you believe?"

"It is what I have found out in one way or another," the Duc replied.

"Then you must have been looking in the wrong place," Lencia said. "Not all women are fickle and, although there are some on whom no sensible man should rely, they are, I would like to believe, the exceptions."

She was thinking of her stepmother as she spoke.

Then she was aware that the Duc was watching her.

"So you have found women you do not trust," he said. "Was your husband unfaithful to you?"

Because she had forgotten that she was supposed to have had a husband, Lencia looked at him in surprise.

Then she looked away.

"That is not the sort of question," she almost whispered, "that you should ask me."

"Why ever not?" the Duc quizzed her.

As she did not answer him, he said after a moment,

"You are very beautiful, Lady Winterton and I cannot believe that any man would be so foolish as to leave you for another woman even if she was as lovely as Aphrodite herself."

Because she was not used to compliments, Lencia felt herself blushing.

She had been very careful when they washed before luncheon to powder her face and she had also applied a little of the rouge on her cheeks.

She had made herself up carefully before they had left the train in case they encountered the Comte.

She felt that, if she looked older, she could make it very clear to him that he was to leave Alice alone.

Now, as she felt her cheeks burning, she turned her head away and the Duc said,

"Many times I have been in England and I have never, and this is the truth, seen anyone as beautiful as you. Where have you been hiding yourself? When your husband was alive, did he keep you locked up in a harem like an Eastern woman so that no other man could ever see you?"

"I have always lived mostly in the country," Lencia told him. "Therefore the things you are trying to talk about have not come into my life."

"Then you have been very fortunate," the Duc said. "The people who have suffered have been those who have been unable to see you until, of course, now."

There was a note in his voice that told her that he was flirting with her.

Lencia thought that she must be very careful not to take his words seriously.

She had always been warned that Frenchmen flirted with every woman they met and she told herself that she would be very stupid if she listened to what the Duc said or thought that he was being in any way serious.

'It is the way he would talk to any woman he is with,' she thought. 'It is only because I am English that I find it embarrassing.'

She recalled her father saying when he talked to her mother about someone they knew,

"Hardly any Englishwoman knows how to accept a compliment."

"Does that refer to me?" the Countess had asked him.

"Never, my precious," the Earl had answered. "You know as well as I do that every man you meet pays you endless compliments and you receive them modestly, sweetly and with an irresistible sense of humour. It tells them that you don't believe they are genuine."

"I believe *your* compliments," the Countess sighed.

"Of course you do," the Earl answered, "because you know that they all come from my heart. I can only go on saying a thousand times that there is no one in the world as beautiful as you."

They looked at each other lovingly and forgot that Lencia was listening to them.

She had been around about twelve years old at the time and it was a conversation that she had never forgotten.

She thought now that she must behave in the same way as her mother had, enjoying any compliments she was paid but at the same time, unless they came from someone she loved, not taking them at all seriously.

She looked at the Duc.

She was aware that he was watching her with an expression in his eyes that made her feel shy.

"How is it possible you can be so beautiful?" he asked. "I thought as you stood there you might well have been Diane de Poitiers her very self. You will remember that she was the most beautiful woman in France in her day."

"I am delighted that you think so," Lencia managed to say, "at the same time I must not allow my head to be turned by compliments from a Frenchman who I am quite sure is a past-master at paying them."

The Duc threw back his head and laughed.

"A perfect answer indeed and a very clever one. I can assure you. Lady Winterton, that it is quite unnecessary for you to be clever as well as beautiful."

They looked at a few more of the superb treasures in Château Chaumont and then the Duc insisted on taking them back to his Château.

"I am not going to allow my guests to become so tired," he said, "that they will refuse to entertain at dinnertime two men who will be waiting for them eagerly to come downstairs."

"I am not the least tired," Alice pointed out firmly. "And I shall be getting up very early tomorrow morning so that I can go again to Château Chaumont."

"I am afraid you will have to wait for us," the Duc said, "because Pierre and I want to ride before breakfast. So that meal is postponed until nine-thirty."

"I suppose you will have some very fine horses," Alice exclaimed.

"I hope that is what they are," the Duc answered.

"Can I see them?" Lencia asked. "I have always heard that French horses are outstanding and, now you have been competing in some of our races, you have been very successful."

The Duc put his hand up to his forehead.

"How could I have been so stupid," he asked, "knowing that you are English not to take you to the stables first before we went to Chaumont?"

He was joking, but Alice insisted,

"Château Chaumont is far more important because we are in France. If we had been in England, it would have been the stables first."

The Duc laughed.

"Now it has to be the stables second and I hope that you will both ride with me tomorrow morning."

Alice looked at Lencia and said,

"Oh, Lencia, why did you not think of it? How could you have been so stupid?"

"What has she done wrong?" the Duc enquired.

"We did not bring our riding clothes," Alice grumbled.

"How could we have possibly known," Lencia asked, "that there were horses and a real Duc waiting for us at Chaumont?"

She spoke in such a despairing tone that the men both laughed.

Then the Duc suggested,

"I am sure my housekeeper can find something you can wear. I have sisters and nieces who stay here often, and I am quite certain they leave behind everything that can possibly be wanted. At seven-thirty in the morning you will be seen only by the horses themselves."

Alice gave a little cry.

"You are wonderful! I know you must have stepped straight out of a Fairytale to help us, because you cannot possibly be real."

"Now at last I have found someone who appreciates me," the Duc said, "but I have a feeling it is only cupboard love."

Alice laughed and then she said,

"I can only say that we are very very grateful and everything is far more exciting than I ever expected."

"Let us hope that continues," the Duc supported her.

When they were back at the Duc's Château, they then went upstairs to their bedrooms and Alice said,

"This is so wonderful, Lencia. Are you not glad that we came?"

"I am very glad," Lencia answered. "But we must still be careful."

"Why?" Alice enquired.

Lencia glanced to make sure that the door was closed and then she said,

"We are staying here without a chaperone, which would be shocking if anyone knew that I am not who I am pretending to be – a widowed lady."

"I never thought of that," Alice remarked. "We will be extra careful."

"I told the Duc just vaguely that I had a house in Kent and it is where I live."

Alice was still for a moment and then she admitted,

"I have a dreadful feeling that, when Pierre asked me, I said that it was in Hampshire."

Lencia made a gesture with her hands.

"We can only hope that being French, they will not be very interested in the Counties of England. But try not to answer any questions like that one directly."

"They are so nice," Alice said, "and I like Pierre very much. I am sure that neither he nor the Duc would do anything to hurt us."

"I think that too," Lencia agreed. "At the same time the Duc is often in England and he may even have met Papa."

"We will be especially careful until we leave," Alice promised. "And after that it will not matter."

Lencia did not reply.

She was thinking how terribly shocked her father and mother's friends would be if they knew that they were staying with the Duc de Montrichard in his Château and unchaperoned.

She did not know anything about him.

She had the feeling that he was a dashing figure who would, of course, know everyone in the Social world.

'We must be very careful,' she reminded herself again.

Equally she was beginning to feel rather frightened.

CHAPTER FOUR

The Duc was right, his housekeeper produced riding clothes for both Lencia and Alice.

They dressed themselves quickly at seven o'clock in the morning.

The housekeeper had even been clever enough to provide boots that actually fitted them.

As the clothes were very French, Lencia had a happy feeling that they were both looking their best for their ride.

She was just leaving her bedroom when she remembered she had not made up her face and then hurried back to do so.

"You look very pretty when your face is painted," Alice said, "and it certainly does make you look older."

"I hope so," Lencia said, "and don't forget that I am many years older than you are."

Alice laughed.

"I will not forget and if they ask me, I will say that you are like a very strict Governess."

"We had better hurry," Lencia urged her, "or we shall be late."

They ran downstairs and found the Duc and Pierre waiting for them in the hall.

"A miracle," the Duc applauded, "two women who are actually on time!"

"If you are surprised, then you must be thinking of French women," Lencia replied. "The English are always very punctual where horses are concerned."

"Well, don't let us keep ours waiting," the Duc said and moved towards the door.

The grooms were holding four horses outside.

Next Lencia was shown the very well-bred stallion that she was to ride.

She was certain that the Duc had chosen it for her because it was well trained and she would have no difficulty in controlling it.

She did not say anything.

When they reached some flat land after riding through the Park, she pushed her horse on.

It was an effort to beat the others, who were all galloping and she was aware as she did so that the Duc was watching her.

When finally they pulled their horses to a standstill, he said,

"I was quite right, I knew, because you are English, you would ride well and also look even more like Diane de Poitiers than when you are on foot."

"You must talk to my sister about Diane," Lencia said. "She is her favourite heroine."

"I am surprised you allow that," the Duc replied, "considering that she was a mistress of King Henry II."

Lencia smiled.

"One is always allowed a little licence when it comes to history. The mistresses of Kings somehow have an aura of mystery about them that does not exist in real life."

The Duc looked at her in surprise and then he queried,

"So what about your Prince of Wales?"

For a moment Lencia was nonplussed.

She had forgotten that the Prince of Wales had caused so much gossip and talk, first with his friendship with Lily Langtry and then later, following after several other great beauties, his adoration for the Countess of Warwick.

She knew, although she said nothing that the Duc was aware of what she was thinking.

After a moment he said,

"Exactly and hardly a good example to innocent young girls like your sister."

Lencia had a feeling that this was a question of 'the pot calling the kettle black'.

However, she thought to say so would seem too familiar and she therefore replied,

"You must not believe all you hear about our Royal Family. Any more than we believe all we hear about the endless gaieties of Paris and the fortunes that are spent on some of your most beautiful women."

"*Touché*," the Duc said. "I see, Lady Winterton, that you have an answer to everything."

"I am afraid that is not true," Lencia replied, "but it is you who has all the answers."

"Perhaps I wanted to see your re-action to the delightful story of Diane and Henry II," the Duc said. "She was very feminine and she loved her protector. With her guidance France became more prosperous than it had ever been before."

"You must tell all this to Alice," Lencia suggested firmly.

"I prefer to talk to you," the Duc replied. "I think, Lady Winterton, we will find that we have a great many things in common and a great many subjects to discuss."

"At the moment I just want to tell you," Lencia said, "how much I am enjoying this ride. But I am well aware, *monsieur*, that you chose me a very quiet and docile horse. Tomorrow, if I am going to ride with you again, I would like one with more spirit and more difficult to control."

"Now you are speaking in the way I expected. I did not believe that under that quiet and dignified manner, which, of course, is most impressive, there was not an adventurous little Goddess wanting to express herself far more vividly."

Lencia thought that he was uncomfortably perceptive and that could lead to trouble.

She then pointed out a little coldly,

"I try to be just myself and not to pretend to be anything else."

"And yourself is the *you* I want to meet," the Duc said, "because she intrigues me. Yet I feel there are barriers that I somehow have to sweep away or surmount first."

Lencia was now aware that he was far more astute than she had expected.

She moved her horse forward and started off in a gallop.

She knew that it prevented the Duc from saying anything further.

She had a feeling that, while he was flirting with her, he was doing it in rather an unusual way.

He was, in fact, rather obviously probing to find out more about her.

They rode for an hour through the most beautiful countryside and the Duc explained that it still harboured a large number of wild animals as it had in the days of King François I in the sixteenth century.

"Stags, wild boar and deer," he told her.

Alice listened when he talked about the local game and the celebrated hunt on his land.

Yet whenever she could, she looked again to see the glorious view of Château Chaumont in the distance.

It was impossible for the Duc and Pierre not to see that she was counting the hours until she could go back there.

When they arrived back at the Château, there was a large breakfast waiting for them in the dining room and they went straight in without changing.

Then, as Alice finished her breakfast first, she said enquiringly,

"What time will we be leaving?"

"I suppose," the Duc replied, "you are bullying me into taking you to Chaumont again. Very well, go and change and I will fetch all my keys and bring them with me."

Alice gave him a ravishing smile.

"I knew you would understand," she said. "I cannot waste time on other things."

"No, of course not," the Duc agreed, "and Pierre and I will make certain that at the end of the day you are so tired that we can all have a rest tomorrow!"

"Now you are being unkind to me," Alice protested vigorously.

She then ran from the dining room and up the stairs.

Lencia left more slowly, feeling that she must behave as an older woman would.

The Duc walked with her into the hall.

"Now go and make yourself look even lovelier than you do at the moment," he said. "I want Château Chaumont to see you."

Lencia laughed.

"I thought it was *we* who are going to see Château Chaumont."

"The Château has seen many beauties," the Duc said, "but I am prepared to wager a large sum of money that the beauty I will be producing today will eclipse them all."

"Be careful, you might lose," Lencia chided him.

"If you challenge me, I shall double my bet," the Duc replied and grinned.

Lencia laughed and went upstairs.

As she did so, she thought how enjoyable it was to duel with words as she did with the Duc.

It was something that she had never been able to do before except in her imagination.

Her father, while she adored being with him, did not really like discussing a subject. He was inclined to turn it into a lecture.

She had a feeling that the Duc enjoyed being provocative just to see the re-action of the person he was speaking to.

'I will certainly give him a run for his money,' she told herself.

The maid was waiting to help her into one of her mother's pretty gowns.

As this particular one was in a pale blue, she felt it did not make her look as old as she should appear.

She therefore lifted her hair a little higher and put two small pearl earrings into her ears that had been left to her by her grandmother in her will.

Her mother had, however, never allowed her to wear them.

"Earrings are not right for young girls," she had insisted.

Lencia had found them when she was packing and it was actually the earrings that made her remember that she must have a Wedding ring.

This had meant that once again she had had to go to her mother's room and looked in her dressing table for her jewel box.

The most important jewels were, of course, kept with the family heirlooms in the safe off the pantry.

This was guarded at night by one of the footmen who slept in the same room.

Their mother had kept a number of small jewels which she wore regularly in her dressing table.as it was too much trouble to keep taking them out of the safe.

Lencia had found her mother's Wedding ring.

Fortunately it fitted onto the finger of her left hand almost as if it had been made for her.

There was also a pearl ring, which she felt she would wear in the evening and a necklace that matched it.

She hesitated about a small but very pretty diamond necklace, thinking, as she and Alice were going to stay in a hotel, that she would not need jewels.

Then, just in case it was necessary, she slipped it into her jewel case.

Now she thought if she wore earrings she would look more like the widowed woman she was supposed to be.

They looked impressive under the hat she was wearing, which was trimmed with velvet flowers and two feathers.

When Alice came in to see if she was ready, she exclaimed,

"Oh, you do look lovely! I am sure that the Duc will think so."

"He says very flattering things," Lencia said, "and I don't believe any of them. If Pierre flatters you, you must remember that for a Frenchman it is the polite way to behave and they forget what they have said the moment they have said it."

"I like having compliments," Alice said, "and it is certainly a change from Englishmen, who talk enthusiastically only about fishing and shooting."

Lencia laughed.

"Well, make the best of it while you can because we shall soon be back home listening to what a success

Stepmama has been in Sweden and all the smart people she has met."

Alice made a face.

"We are sure to have to listen to that and if anyone exciting or interesting comes to the house, we shall doubtless be sent to the schoolroom and told to stay there."

Lencia thought that this was very likely.

She felt it justified her in having brought Alice to France without her father's permission.

"Oh, do come on," Alice was saying. "We are now wasting time talking about what we are going to do at home when we are here in France and the doors of Château Chaumont are going to open for us."

She went out of the room as she spoke.

Lencia took one last look at herself in the golden mirror and then followed her.

The carriage was waiting for them outside.

The Duc and Lencia sat on the back seat while Alice and Pierre sat opposite with their backs to the horses.

They were talking nineteen to the dozen.

Lencia knew all that mattered to Alice was that she was on her way to Chaumont.

When they reached it, the Duc took them into it by a different door from the one he had used the previous day.

It was to the main section of the Château and had four great guard rooms laid out in the shape of a Greek Cross.

From there he took them up a staircase with windows that led out onto a terrace.

From there they were able to see tangled chimneys, dormer windows, newel staircases, steeples and pepper pot roofs.

He explained to them that this was once a fantastic vantage point and from it the ladies of the Court could watch entertainments such as hunts, tournaments or parades.

"It was used occasionally for balls," Pierre added.

Alice gave a little cry.

"Oh, do give a ball!" she said to the Duc. "Think how exciting it would be for everyone and you could watch your guests from here and feel that you were King François bringing the Château to life."

"I think I would rather give a ball in my own house," the Duc answered. "It is something, Pierre, you and I might consider for later on in this summer."

"I have never been to a ball," Alice said. "Perhaps if I am still not old enough to come to yours, I can watch it from a place like this."

"If I give a ball and you are in France," the Duc said, "then you shall be one of my most honoured guests."

Alice jumped for joy.

Then, as she caught Lencia's eyes, she remembered that, even if she was invited to the ball, she would not be able to go.

They would never be able to explain to their father how they were friends of the Duc's.

For a moment the excitement went out of her eyes and she turned without speaking and began to descend from the terrace.

The others followed and Lencia said nothing.

She was, however, quite certain that the Duc was aware that he had somehow trodden on unsafe ground and it was something that he would not forget.

They reached the ground floor.

When they opened a locked door and stepped through it, they found themselves in a part of the Château that was open to the public.

A number of people were being taken round by a guide with a squeaky voice.

Behind them and clearly not one of the group was, to Lencia's consternation, the Comte.

He saw Alice, who was still a little ahead and then he walked swiftly towards her.

"Where have you been?" he asked her. "I looked for you yesterday and I felt sure that I should find you here."

Before Alice could reply, the Duc, who had come through the door last, said in a lofty tone,

"Miss Austin was with me, Pontlevoy, and I am showing her round The Château."

The Comte started and looked at the Duc in a hostile fashion.

"I had promised to show Miss Austin the Château myself," he said angrily.

"Which, of course, you are not able to do. She is seeing with me the locked rooms and the parts of the Château that are not open to the public."

He made the last words sound like a deliberate insult.

The Comte then growled,

"I might have guessed that you would somehow interfere."

"It is not a question of interference," the Duc said. "Lady Winterton and her sister are my guests and I can assure you that they will be well looked after and need no assistance from anyone else."

"That," the Comte said, "is exactly the sort of remark that I should expect from Monsieur Mille-Feuilles.

It was now obvious that he had lost his temper and was being offensively rude.

"Then you have not been disappointed," the Duc said coldly.

As he spoke, he took Lencia by the arm and moved towards another door that he had the key for.

He unlocked it.

Alice and Pierre followed him and Lencia through it.

The Duc then slammed the door intentionally and locked it on the inside.

"I am so glad you have got rid of him," Lencia sighed.

"Perhaps he intends only to be kind," Alice objected, "and he did talk about Chaumont as if he was very fond of it."

"I doubt if he would have been so attentive," the Duc said, "if you had not been a very pretty young girl.

So forget the Comte and, I can assure you, you will never meet him in my house."

Alice did not reply.

A few moments later, when she was racing Pierre up the stairs, Lencia, who was going more slowly, turned to the Duc.

"Thank you for getting rid of that man. I knew he was horrible as soon as he spoke to us on the ferry to Calais."

"Forget him," the Duc answered. "He dislikes me because I refuse to know him even though he lives in the neighbourhood and he spreads very unpleasant stories about me, which I am glad to say few people believe."

"He called you 'Monsieur Mille-Feuilles'," Lencia said. "Why did he do that?"

The Duc smiled a little cynically.

"I would have thought that it was obvious."

"A thousand leaves," she translated.

"Perhaps he should have said 'Mille-Fleurs',"

Lencia thought for a moment and then she queried,

"You mean a thousand women. Is that how they describe you?"

The Duc made a gesture with his hands.

"Shall we say there is some slight exaggeration."

There was a silence and then Lencia quizzed him,

"And that makes you happy?"

"I find women very attractive especially if they are beautiful," the Duc said. "Can you blame a man for not refusing what the Gods offer him?"

"Yet you said," Lencia re-joined, "like King François that '*a woman is fickle*'."

"I think in their way they are as fickle as men," the Duc said. "But it is not so easy for them to move from flower to flower as it is for a man."

They had reached a room where there was some very attractive old furniture.

Then almost without thinking what she was doing, Lencia sat down on the sofa.

"Why have you never married?" she asked.

"But I have," the Duc replied.

Lencia was surprised, but she did not quite know why.

He had not seemed to her to be like a married man.

"I was married and, of course, it was an arranged marriage," he said. "As you know in France it is usual between great families. I was just twenty-one and I was told that she was beautiful. When I saw her I admitted that she was certainly pretty, but there was something strange about her that I did not quite understand."

Lencia was listening to him intently.

She knew by the tone of his voice that it hurt him to speak of what had happened.

"As I said," he went on, "my father and her father arranged the marriage. I saw very little of my future bride and, of course, never alone until after the Wedding."

"Then what happened?" Lencia asked.

"When I was on my honeymoon," the Duc said, "my wife, who had been so carefully chosen for me, did not behave normally. She was given to strange fits of screaming, which usually ended in her becoming unconscious."

Lencia made a little exclamation of horror, but she did not speak and the Duc continued,

"At first they occurred no more than once a month and then became more frequent. I sent for the doctors, who informed me that my wife was mentally deranged. I also learned that her parents had known about it before they arranged the marriage with me."

Lencia gave a cry.

"But how terrible! How could they do such a thing?"

"They wanted her to become the Duchesse of Montrichard and so nothing else was of any importance."

"It was ghastly for you," Lencia said. "What did you do about it?"

"Because I was ashamed of being duped, I tried to keep it a secret. But my wife became worse and worse. Finally she was taken away to a hospital and she died a year later and, as you can understand, it was a merciful release. But I never did forgive those who had deceived me."

Now he spoke bitterly and Lencia said,

"I can understand. It must have been terrible for you and you were too young to really cope with it."

"Much too young then. I went to Paris and found that a young man could enjoy himself without being afflicted by being tied to one woman. It made me very determined that I would never marry again."

"I can appreciate that," Lencia said, "and I am so very sorry for you."

"There is no need for you to be," the Duc replied. "As Monsieur Mille-Feuilles I have enjoyed every moment of the last six years. I am a free man and it is how I intend to remain."

"Of course," Lencia agreed, "but one day you will fall in love."

There was a twist to the Duc's mouth as he answered,

"Do you really think that I have not been in love already?"

"I am quite certain you have not," Lencia said, "or you would not be talking the way you are now. When you do fall in love, as you will one day, you will find it is very different from the amusements of Paris and the fickle women who you have tried to rely on."

"Now I suppose you are being prophetic or else clairvoyant," the Duc smiled.

"I am just telling you the truth," Lencia said. "When you do fall in love, you will realise that I have told you the truth."

"But suppose it never happens," the Duc retorted.

He did not wait for her to answer, but went on,

"So often I have said to myself, 'this is different, this is going to be something that I have never felt before.' But always the end comes in the same way and, to put it very frankly, I am bored."

"That is because you have never been really in love." Lencia suggested.

She was thinking of how her father had fallen in love with her mother and how happy they had been all through the years they had been together.

"I do believe," she said slowly, "that one falls in love when one meets what the Ancient Greeks called 'the other half of oneself'. Then there is no doubt that this is the one person in the world that you have been seeking."

"Is that what you found?" the Duc enquired.

Without thinking, because she was concentrating on him and not on herself, Lencia told the truth,

"No, but I hope and pray it will happen to me and I feel sure that one day it will."

It was only then she realised what she had said and rose to her feet.

"But we were talking about you," she said, "and that is what is important. So promise me that you will carry on seeking just as Jason sought the Golden Fleece. All men in their hearts want to follow a star."

She did not know why those words came to her lips, but they did.

Then she moved over the room to stand at the balcony, looking out over the beauty of the surrounding countryside.

It was some seconds before the Duc joined her and then he said,

"Now I find you more mysterious and even more difficult to understand than you were before."

"I am not important," Lencia said. "I am only 'a ship that passes in the night'. What you have to think about is yourself and your own future."

"I have done that for quite some time," the Duc said. "Then another leaf comes fluttering at my feet and once again I am optimistic."

"That is what you must continue to be because, as I promised you, one day your dreams will all come true."

The Duc was about to reply when Alice and Pierre came back into the room.

"We have been right up to the roof," Alice said, "and I am sure I saw a wild boar move among the trees."

"Well, don't you go too near to it," the Duc warned. "They can be very fierce, especially when there are a number of them together."

"I would be far too frightened to go into the woods at night," Alice said. "Even at home they are rather creepy after the sun has gone down. You can hear the rabbits scratching in the undergrowth and the deer suddenly move when one least expects it."

"Much better to stay indoors and look for the ghosts," Pierre joked.

"We don't have ghosts in our – "

Alice stopped.

She was just about to say 'Castle' when she caught her sister's eye.

After a second's pause, Alice added rather lamely,

" – house."

"Well, there are lots of them in Uncle Valaire's Château," Pierre said, "so you had better be careful that you do not run into one when you least expect it.

You might see one staring down at you when you are lying in bed."

"Now you really are frightening me," Alice cried.

"Pay no attention to him," the Duc said. "I will not have all this nonsense about ghosts for the simple reason that some women are really terrified by them."

"I expect it is when they hear people tramping about the passages," Pierre added.

Now he was looking at his uncle in a provocative manner.

"If you are going to be impertinent," the Duc said, "I shall send you away tomorrow or forbid you to ride my horses."

"No! *no*!" Pierre cried at once, "I apologise."

Now he was speaking theatrically so that they all had to laugh.

"I am certain that it would be the worst punishment of all," Lencia said, "if you locked up your horses and just went riding by yourself."

"It was a punishment that I suffered as a small boy," the Duc said, "and one that I shall certainly administer to Pierre if he grows too cheeky."

"I promise I shall speak of you only in the kindest and most adulatory manner," Pierre retorted. "You cannot condemn me to run round the Château shouting, '*A horse, a horse, my Kingdom for a horse*!'"

"I am sure he would not be so cruel," Alice said, "when he has been so kind as to bring me here. And please, can I see more of Château Chaumont?"

The Duc looked at his watch.

"I think we should go back to luncheon," he proposed. "I will take you a different way in case we meet any unpleasant characters, who in my opinion are more trouble than ghosts."

They all knew that he was speaking of the Comte de Pontlevoy.

Lencia thought that it would be a great mistake to meet him and give him the opportunity of being as disagreeable as he had been before.

They then left the Château by one of the doors that only the Duc had a key for and found the carriage without further incident.

They drove back to the Château Richard, where there was a delicious luncheon waiting for them.

It was quite late before they finally left the dining room after plenty of fascinating talk.

"What I would like now," Pierre announced, "is a game of tennis. Will you play with me, Uncle Valaire?"

"What about our guests?" the Duc enquired.

"We both play tennis," Lencia volunteered, "and I hope we are good enough for you."

"Go and find some comfortable shoes," the Duc suggested, "and we shall soon find out how good you are."

As they ran up the stairs, Alice commented,

"You are very good at tennis, Lencia."

"And you have improved a great deal in the last year," Lencia said. "Anyway it is good exercise and, if we get in their way, it is just their own fault."

"They are so nice," Alice sighed, "and I was so glad today that I was not caught by that Comte. He was trying to be very rude to the Duc. What could he have meant by calling him 'Monsieur Mille-Feuilles?'

"I expect it is just a French way of being rude," Lencia replied.

They found that the two men were very good at tennis, but managed to keep their end up.

Lencia served unusually well for a woman because she had had plenty of lessons.

When they were all exhausted, they lay down in the grass under the trees.

The Duc then ordered a delicious fruit cup to be brought out for them, which was very refreshing when they were so hot.

"We certainly did not expect all this to happen when we left England," Alice remarked, "and I cannot help wondering what we will do next,"

"I will tell you what we will do after dinner," Pierre said. "We will play Uncle Valaire's new phonograph and I will dance with you unless you are very heavy on your feet."

"Now you are being insulting," Alice said, "I am longing to see a phonograph as I have never seen one before."

"If you lived with my uncle," Pierre replied, "you would realise that he always has the very latest gadgets available."

Lencia looked at the Duc.

"Is that true?" she asked him.

"I try," he said. "It bores me to read about things in the newspapers and not be able to utilise them for myself."

"I have read a great deal about the phonograph and how it works," Lencia pointed out.

"Actually Pierre does not realise that I have just bought a Berliner gramophone."

"That is even more exciting," Lencia exclaimed.

"I think it is one of the novelties that will be improved a great deal in the coming years," the Duc informed her. "Tomorrow I want to show you another new acquisition that I have been working on for some time."

"What is that?" Lencia enquired.

"It is a motorboat that I have built so that it can navigate the Loire which, as perhaps you know, is very shallow."

"That will be exciting," Lencia smiled

Then in a low voice she added,

"You are so kind to have us here. It has made a wonderful holiday for my sister."

"And I hope for you," the Duc said

"I am very thrilled by everything I see and happier to be here than I could ever put into words."

"That is what I want you to say," the Duc answered. "For my part it has given me a great deal of pleasure to have you as my guests. You so much enhance the beauty of the Château which I have always thought very lovely in itself."

Once again he was complimenting her and Lencia managed to smile and not blush.

"How long have you been out of mourning?" the Duc next asked her.

Thinking of her mother and forgetting that he was talking about her mythical husband, Lencia said,

"The twelve months finished a month ago so we need no longer wear black."

"I think with your hair and your skin," the Duc mused meditatively, "that black would make you look somewhat theatrical but, of course, no less lovely."

"I prefer pale colours and now that I can go to balls, I shall have some very pretty gowns in pale blue and perhaps pink."

"In which you will look like a rosebud," the Duc said. "Or should I say a rose in bloom?"

"The rose in bloom is, of course, more correct," Lencia responded quickly.

"I am not at all certain that is right," the Duc rejoined. "There is something very young about you. In fact I find it difficult to believe that you are much more than twenty."

Lencia gave an affected little laugh.

"Now you are certainly paying me compliments. I suppose that no woman likes to think that she looks her real age."

"It depends how old she is," the Duc said. "But I am telling you that there is something very young about you and I feel that you are hardly any older than Alice."

Lencia laughed again.

"I suppose we would all like to put back the clock. But think, if I was a *debutante*, how bored you would be in talking to me."

"Why should you think that?" the Duc asked.

"As I have always been told that dashing young gentlemen like yourself find *debutantes* very boring and, of course, they are frightened that they will be dragged up the aisle, which is the ambition of every *debutante's* pushy mother."

Perhaps it was something she should not have said after their conversation that morning.

The Duc, however, replied,

"Perhaps you are right. I suppose that is the English point of view, but it does not trouble a Frenchman so much."

"You mean because they have arranged marriages?" Lencia suggested.

"That is quick of you," he said approvingly. "A man does not have to look for his first wife, his parents do it for him."

"I think it is a horrible idea," Lencia asserted, "and look what happened to you."

"Something like that happens once in a million times," the Duc said. "All the same it is right that blue blood should go to blue blood. As you know, the French are very proud about their ancestry and so fussy that it should not be soiled in any way by an unfortunate liaison."

"It is the same with Royalty," Lencia said. "That is, of course, why we forgive Kings like Charles II and, as you pointed out this morning, our Prince of Wales, looking for amusements outside their Palaces."

"With often disastrous results," the Duc said. "I think your idea of meeting someone with whom one at once falls madly and crazily but permanently in love is far more satisfactory but unfortunately it very seldom happens in real life."

"One day it will happen to you," Lencia said. "As I told you this morning, you are not to feel that your life is not as perfect as you would want it to be. You are still young and I am quite certain that your Guardian Angel in Heaven is looking after you and so will bring the right woman to you."

She spoke with a sincerity that was somehow rather touching.

The Duc put out his hand and laid it over hers.

"This is the first time," he said, "that anyone has said that to me and I am very grateful to you."

Lencia smiled at him.

Then she was aware that because his hand was touching hers, a little thrill ran through her.

She could not explain it in any way to herself.

She only knew that it was something very special that she had never felt before.

CHAPTER FIVE

That evening after dinner Pierre and Alice danced to the gramophone.

The Duc, however, claimed that he did not have the right records.

"I am making plans for tomorrow," he said just before they went off to bed. "And I have an idea that I think you will all enjoy."

They looked at him attentively and he went on,

"First of all we will not ride before breakfast, which is rather tiring, but in the morning. Then, after luncheon, I want to show you my motorboat, which I think is totally unique."

"I would love to," Lencia enthused.

"I am afraid that Alice may be a little disappointed," the Duc continued, "but I promise her that the following day we will visit at least three Châteaux, which will keep her happy for a long time."

"Three will be exciting," Alice said, "even though tomorrow will be a bit of a wasted day."

They all laughed at her for saying this and the Duc then said,

"Perhaps, Alice, you will forgive me when I tell you that tomorrow night I have arranged for someone to come and play real music for us to dance to."

Alice clasped her hands together.

"A ball all of our very own," she exclaimed.

"Exactly," the Duc went on. "Just a little ball for you and me and we hope the rest of the party will enjoy it."

Alice moved impulsively towards him and without thinking laid her cheek against his shoulder.

"You are so kind to us," she sighed, "I don't know how to thank you."

"Thank me by both of you looking very beautiful tomorrow night," the Duc proposed.

When they went up to bed, Alice was talking excitedly about being able to dance to what the Duc had called 'real music'.

She had almost forgotten that she would miss her beloved Château Chaumont for one day.

*

Lencia found it rather pleasant to rise much later the next morning and luxuriate in her comfortable bed for at least an extra hour.

She went down to breakfast in her riding habit.

"There is so much of my estate that I want to show you," the Duc said when they rose from the table. "I think you will find it particularly lovely and, if Alice is lucky, she should see a wild boar."

They set off for quite a long ride.

Lencia thought that the Duc had underestimated the beauty of their surroundings, which she found breathtaking.

The woods, the pasture land and the views were lovelier than any countryside that she had ever seen before or imagined.

"This is Fairyland," she said to the Duc, "and I think you are very lucky to live in it."

"That is what I think myself," he replied, "and why I try to make my Château as perfect as it is possible for it to be."

"I have been looking at your treasures," Lencia said, "and I can understand how much they mean to you."

"Most of them are beautiful, like you and I should mind losing them just as any man who owned you would be desperate if he lost you."

He was obviously flirting with her again.

At the same time Lencia felt that he spoke with a sincerity that was difficult to ignore.

She tried to change the subject, but the Duc said,

"I was wondering if there is anything you don't do well. You ride better than any woman I have ever seen, you play tennis very well and, of course, you make every man's heart turn a somersault as soon as he sees you."

Lencia just smiled and he carried on,

"What I am longing to know is what it is that makes your heart throb quicker and why your marriage was not a success."

"Who said it was not a success?" Lencia enquired.

"You told me that you had not found the perfect love, which you promised I would find one day. So after you married you were obviously disappointed."

"I don't want to talk about it," Lencia replied quickly.

She pressed her horse forward and the Duc called after her,

"You cannot go on running away and you know as well as I do, Lencia, I am intensely curious about you."

She had noticed that he had used her Christian name last night for the first time, but then thought that it would be a mistake to challenge it.

Instead she said,

"If you knew all there is to know, you would be bored, and therefore, Monsieur Mille-Feuilles, I only hope that I can keep you guessing."

She was speaking lightly because she felt that it was the only way that she could answer him.

To her surprise the Duc said seriously,

"Do you mean that? Are you really eager to keep me where I am at the moment – at your feet?"

Lencia turned her head away.

Despite her resolution not to be moved by him, she could not help feeling a little tremor run through her.

Then she told herself that he was a Frenchman and she must not believe anything he said to her.

"I am waiting for an answer," the Duc persisted after a short silence.

"Perhaps it is good for you to wait," Lencia said. "I am sure that all the lovely *fleurs* you met in Paris fell into your arms the moment you appeared."

"Now you are just guessing," the Duc said. "Although I like a puzzle, I want to be very confident that I can solve it in the last chapter."

"And if you fail?" Lencia asked.

"Then like the ghosts in the Château, you will haunt me."

Lencia thought that was indeed possible.

When they went back to England without his knowing who she was, there would be no chance of their ever seeing each other again.

"The answer to what you are thinking," he said, "is that if you leave me in ignorance, I shall always feel that by my sheer stupidity I have lost something irreplaceable."

"No one could accuse you of that," Lencia answered. "At the same time the answer to some questions are rather like the stars – out of reach."

She moved forward before the Duc could reply.

It was, she told herself, becoming difficult to carry on keeping him in ignorance of who they were and where they really came from.

When they returned for luncheon, Pierre talked about the motorboat.

"It was entirely due to Uncle Valaire," he said proudly, "that the barges moving on the Loire and the canals around here are now using Priestman engines. It makes them go faster and in that way save a lot of money."

"How clever of you," Lencia exclaimed. "I am sure that no one else has ever thought of having engines in barges."

"On the contrary they tried it in England first," the Duc replied. "But it was a Keystone engine craft, ahead of its time in having high-tension ignition."

As he finished speaking, he laughed.

"You will not understand what I am saying, but I am quite prepared to take the credit for having introduced the Priestman engines to France, which have proved a great success I am happy to report."

"And that, I suppose, is the engine your motorboat has," Lencia said a little tentatively.

"You are quite right," the Duc replied, "and I had to have something very simple to use on the Loire because it is so shallow, flowing between sandbanks on either side. If you move from the centre of the river, you get into trouble unless your boat is of very shallow draught."

"I understand," Lencia nodded, "I am longing to see your motorboat."

"It really is completely unique," Pierre said, "until that ghastly Comte of Alice's copied Uncle Valaire."

"He is not 'my' Comte," Alice protested. "I think he is horrible and I hope we don't see him ever again."

"Did he really copy your motorboat?" Lencia enquired.

"He did, as he has copied so many other ideas of mine," the Duc admitted, "but there is nothing I can do about it."

"The Comte uses his boat for very different purposes than Uncle Valaire uses his," Pierre announced. "He has built a sort of hood over it like on a chaise so that he can sit inside it with a girl and not be seen."

"Stop talking about him," the Duc commanded, "and let's go down to the river now. The carriage is waiting."

They climbed into the carriage and drove down to the banks of the Loire.

Its course was almost straight where it flowed through the Duc's land and they could see it glittering away into the far distance towards Orleans.

Because the river was so low, the sandbanks were visible on either side of it and Lencia could understand how important it was to have a boat that would not go aground.

The Duc was expected and the motorboat was ready outside the boathouse.

As it was the first one that she had ever seen, Lencia was thrilled at the sight of it.

It was in fact somewhat smaller than she might have expected with two seats in front and two behind.

They inspected it and were about to get into it, when the Duc turned to Lencia,

"I want to show you the inside of the boathouse. I have invented also a special way of lifting up the boat so that the hull can be cleaned easily underneath after it has a lot of sand sticking to it. It is a lift, which I don't think anyone else has thought of so far."

"I would love to see it," Lencia said.

They went into the boathouse while Pierre and Alice walked a little way along the side of the river.

He was throwing stones and showing her how by sleight of hand he could make them jump along the surface of the water.

"Oh! I must try that," Alice said and went down to the edge of the bank.

The lift was as the Duc had described it and his man who was in charge of the boat and the boathouse demonstrated how the machine worked to raise the boat out of the river.

"I do think it is clever of you," Lencia said, "and, of course, I can understand that, when the water is very low, it is impossible for the hull not to become clogged with sand."

"I sometimes wish I lived on a deeper river," the Duc admitted, "but at the same time I love the Loire. It has a beauty all of its own and, if it gives us problems, then obviously one has to solve them."

"As you do most effectively," Lencia added.

He smiled at her and then suddenly Pierre came bursting into the boathouse.

"Uncle Valaire! *Uncle Valaire!*" he cried out. "The Comte has kidnapped Alice!"

"What do you mean?" the Duc asked him sharply.

"He came along in his boat, saw us and asked Alice if he could give her a ride. Although she refused, he threw a rope ashore and made fast to a stake on the riverbank. When she told him again she did not want to go with him, he said, 'very well, Pierre, loosen the rope for me otherwise I cannot move away'."

Pierre, who was breathless, paused before he carried on,

"While I went to do so, the Comte lifted Alice into the boat, released the rope and drove off!"

"How awful! How dreadful!" Lencia cried.

The Duc walked towards the door.

"Quickly," he urged, "I shall be able to overtake him if we hurry."

Lencia and Pierre both ran and jumped into the motorboat followed by the Duc.

Pierre sat behind and Lencia next to the Duc.

His man released the ropes holding it and next the Duc started up the engine.

With a roar they began moving up the river.

"Do you know where – he has – gone?" Lencia asked, having to raise her voice above the noise of the engine.

"I imagine the devil will take her to his Château," the Duc replied, "which is a little way up the river beyond Chaumont."

The Duc spoke sharply and there was a grim look in his eyes that told Lencia that he was very angry.

She guessed that it was not entirely because he wanted Alice that the Comte had carried her away so outrageously.

He very obviously hated the Duc and wanted to hurt him in any way he could.

At the same time she was very worried about Alice, knowing how frightened she would be.

'Why,' she asked herself, 'did we ever come on this trip? If we had stayed at home, there would have been no unpleasant Comte to behave in such an appalling way.'

But she could not help thinking that there would also have been no kind charming and resourceful Duc.

Then she forced herself to think only of Alice.

If the Comte was alone in his motorboat, he could hardly frighten her by trying to kiss her. Anything like that was out of the question while he was manipulating his boat.

It was therefore essential that the Duc should overtake him before he could reach his own Château.

"How fast can – you go?" she asked him nervously.

"Faster than the Comte can manage in his boat," the Duc replied. "He thought he was copying me exactly, but I found out from Priestman that he had squeezed down the price and so they had not given him exactly the same horsepower as they had given me."

Lencia looked ahead, but could not see any sign of the Comte's boat.

The Duc was in the centre of the river, driving his engine forwards to the utmost of its power.

There were, however, three people in his boat and only two in the Comte's.

What was more the Comte was considerably shorter and lighter than the Duc.

Pierre, who was a strongly built young man must, Lencia thought, weigh a great deal.

She then clasped her hands together and prayed.

'Please God, let us overtake him, please God, *please*,' she prayed fervently.

Then, as the Duc glanced at her, she knew that he was aware of what she was doing.

"Don't worry," he said, "we will save her all right. I only hope that I can prevent myself from killing that man, which is something I have wanted to do for a long time."

"I feel the same," Lencia said, "but please be careful. It would cause a terrible scandal if you did kill him."

She was thinking that because the Duc had such a famous name, a fight between the two men would undoubtedly be reported in the newspapers and there would be questions as to who were accompanying them.

As they had English names, false or otherwise, the English newspapers might take up the story.

It could easily happen.

If then it was discovered who Lady Winterton and Miss Austin really were, she could not imagine what would be said by their relations and friends.

"Please – please go faster," she encouraged the Duc.

Behind them Pierre gave a shout.

"There they are!" he called out. "I can see them quite clearly."

Lencia could now see them as well.

A small motorboat was moving up the centre of the river.

Now the Duc was pushing his boat as hard as he could and gradually they drew nearer and nearer to the Comte.

They could see his head bobbing above the cover he had placed over the back seats of his motorboat.

Lencia wondered whether Alice was inside or sitting beside him. Whichever it was there was no sign of her.

The Comte was now becoming aware that they were overtaking him.

A few minutes later the two motorboats were level.

Now, to Lencia's surprise, the Duc was bumping his boat heavily against the Comte's.

At the first bump the Comte shouted,

"Get off and keep away from me!"

Again the Duc moved in and was banging against the side of the Comte's boat so that it was forced a foot or so over to the left.

Again the Comte screeched at them.

It was, however, difficult to hear what he was saying above the loud noise of the engines.

Then, as Lencia waited for the next impact, she understood what the Duc was now doing.

He was forcing the Comte away from the centre of the river towards the sandbanks.

In some places the sandbanks were below the surface of the water, but they were still most definitely there. And they made the river impassable to any craft that did not keep to the centre of it.

Bang – bang – and bang again.

This time the Comte's boat ran onto a sandbank and could not move any further forward.

The Duc then gave it another bang to make quite certain that it was stuck fast in the sand.

As the Comte stood up shouting and swearing, Lencia bent over the side of the boat to look for Alice.

She was on the seat at the back of the Comte's boat and was obviously terrified by what was happening.

It was then that Pierre acted.

The Comte, standing up in his boat, was so enraged that his face was now crimson.

He was leaning forward to try and .make himself heard above the roar of the engines.

Before the Comte could realise what was happening, Pierre had jumped onto his boat and pushed him over the side straight into the river.

He then pulled Alice up from the back seat and held her in his arms.

As the Duc steadied his motorboat, Pierre lifted her into it.

There was just one precarious moment before he joined her, but he managed to spring over the heaving gap between the boats.

The Duc then turned his boat round slowly and carefully so that they could go back the way they had come.

As he did so, Lencia saw that the Comte was standing by his now-useless boat up to his waist in water.

He was shaking his fist at them and shouting.

He was obviously cursing them, but fortunately they could not hear what he was saying.

As the Duc started off down the river, Lencia turned round to ask Alice,

"Are you all right, dearest? He has not hurt you?"

Alice had Pierre's arms around her and raised her head from his shoulder to say,

"I am all right, but I was very – very – frightened."

"Of course you were," Pierre said, "but you must have known that Uncle Valaire would save you."

"I prayed that – you would – come," Alice said, "but I could – not see and, when I – begged the Comte to – stop, he did not hear – me."

"He did not want to," Pierre said. "You are not the first girl he has kidnapped like this."

"I will certainly speak to the Chief of Police about him," the Duc said grimly. "This sort of behaviour cannot go on."

"But – you saved me," Alice said, "and thank – you very much. I felt sure you – would do so, but I – could not help being – frightened. He is such a – nasty man."

"Well, it is going to take him some time to get his motorboat off that sandbank," Pierre commented, "and I hope he catches a bad cold."

"It was clever of you to throw him overboard," the Duc said. "At the same time if he had hit his head and knocked himself out, we would have had to rescue him."

"Personally I would gladly have let him drown," Pierre grinned.

"That would have been asking too much of Fate," the Duc replied, "but I think for the moment he has learned his lesson. No man likes being made to look a complete fool."

The Duc drove the motorboat back to the boathouse.

They then started to walk back across rough ground to where their carriage was waiting for them.

As they did so, a little boy came running through the trees.

He was chasing a rabbit which disappeared into the undergrowth in front of him.

As it did, the boy tripped over a large stone and fell to the ground.

Before anyone else could move, the Duc reached him and picked him up.

The small boy had given a scream and now he was crying.

"You must be very brave," the Duc said. "You have not hurt yourself and the little rabbit has gone away."

The boy's tears stopped.

Because the Duc was holding him high in his arms, he looked at him with interest.

"I very much wanted to catch that rabbit," he said.

"I think it would have been too quick for you," the Duc answered. "But I tell you what you can do, you can go and buy yourself some sweets at the nearest shop and I will give you the money to do so."

The child was all smiles and at that moment his mother appeared.

She was carrying a baby in her arms and, as she hurried up to them, Lencia said to her,

"It is all right. Your son tripped up and fell down, but he is not hurt."

"I think he has scratched his knee," the Duc informed her. "He fell against a stone and it is bleeding a little."

"I will soon stop it, *monsieur*," the mother said.

The Duc sat down on a fallen tree trunk and put the boy on his knee.

Now Lencia could see that it was not a bad cut.

"Let me hold the baby," he asked the mother.

The woman handed him the small baby and he brought a clean handkerchief out of his pocket.

The baby must have been no more than three weeks old. It was a pretty child with just a few dark hairs on its head and large dark eyes.

Its shawl was spotlessly clean and Lencia was certain that the mother looked after both her children well.

The woman now hurried towards the Duc, who was showing a silver coin to the little boy.

When she saw who he was, she curtseyed and said,

"I'm ever so sorry that my son has inconvenienced you, Monsieur le Duc."

"I think he has inconvenienced himself," the Duc replied. "He was chasing a rabbit and you will never stop a small boy doing that."

The woman quickly wiped the trickles of blood from the boy's knee and the Duc put him down on the ground.

"What is his name?" he asked.

There was a little pause and then the woman answered,

"I hope, *monsieur*, you'll not think it impertinent, but we christened him after you."

"I am very honoured," the Duc said, "I do hope that Valaire will grow up to be a strong young man like my nephew. Does your husband work for me?"

"Yes indeed, *monsieur*, he is one of the woodmen."

"Then tell him I am very pleased that his son is interested in the woods already and, of course, there will be a place for him in them when he grows up."

"Thank you, *monsieur*, thank you," the woman said.

The Duc rose from the tree trunk where he had been sitting.

He handed the small boy the coin of silver that he had been showing him and suggested,

"This is for you to buy some sweets."

He took another coin from his pocket, which Lencia thought was a gold Louis.

"And this," he said, "is to buy a present for your mother. You must always, as you grow older, give your mother presents, because she loves you and looks after you."

"I'll do that," the small boy said.

The Duc put his hand on the boy's head and then he said,

"When you do manage to catch a rabbit, tell your father to tell me about it."

"Yes, *monsieur*," the small boy replied.

He was, however, looking at both the coins with delight.

His mother came back and Lencia told her,

"This is a beautiful baby. Is it a boy or a girl?"

"A girl, *madame*," the woman told her.

"Have you had her Christened yet?" the Duc asked.

"She's bein' Christened next Sunday in the Church, *monsieur*."

"Then I will give her one of her names," the Duc said. "Don't forget it. It is 'Lencia'."

"That's a very pretty name Monsieur le Duc, and I'll not forget it," the woman sighed.

She took the baby from Lencia and managed to curtsey to the Duc.

He bade her 'good day' and, taking Lencia by the arm, he helped her up the last steps that led onto the road.

"Now we have two people bearing our names," he said, "and I wonder what their lives will be like."

"If they are as fortunate as we are, very very happy," Lencia answered.

"How can you be sure that it applies to us?" the Duc enquired.

There was no time to answer him as the carriage drew up beside them.

Alice and Pierre had been waiting for them on the road and then they drove back to the Château.

Lencia noticed that the Duc made himself very pleasant to Alice and it was as if he was reassuring her after being so upset and frightened.

'He is very kind and considerate,' Lencia thought to herself.

And she was also very touched by the way that he had treated the small son of one of his woodmen.

'I feel sure that all the people on his estate adore him,' she mused.

They had a delicious tea and then the Duc and Pierre said that they were going to play billiards.

This gave Lencia an opportunity to rest before dinner.

She had in fact, although she told herself that it was stupid, been considerably upset by what had happened to Alice.

She thought too that Alice was looking pale.

"Have a little sleep," she said, "then we will be sparkling at dinner. Don't forget that the Duc has engaged someone to play for us so that we can dance afterwards. It is to be in the Music Room, because the ballroom is too big."

"It will be so exciting to dance with Pierre," Alice enthused. "Even if it is not a real ball, at least we shall not have any competition."

Lencia smiled.

"And we are bound to have a partner for every dance," she smiled.

Alice laughed and then she said,

"Wear Mama's best dress tonight. You may not have another chance and it is so pretty."

Lencia had not thought about it.

Now it seemed to her a sensible thing to do, having brought it all the way to France.

When she put it on, she realised that it was extremely becoming.

Yet because it was made of such soft material and had quite a low *décolleté*, it made her appear very young.

She wore the diamond necklace and the earrings that went with it.

"You look wonderful!" Alice exclaimed when she came into her bedroom. "Pierre has sent me up some flowers, which the maid has arranged in my hair."

They made Alice look very pretty.

It gave a finishing touch to her white gown in which she hoped, if she was allowed to, to come to one of the *debutante* dances that were to be given for her sister.

"No one can say we are not dressed in our best," Lencia said as they walked downstairs. "I only hope that the two gentlemen who are waiting for us will appreciate the effort we have made on their behalf."

"I am sure they will," Alice murmured. "It is just so wonderful to be here dancing with Pierre when I might have been – "

"Don't think about it," Lencia said sharply, knowing what Alice was about to say. "You know very well we would have rescued you even if he had taken you as far as his Château."

"Pierre was very brave to push him in the river and lift me into the Duc's boat," Alice said as if she was re-living the whole chain of events.

Lencia gave a little sigh.

If Alice was to fall in love with Pierre, it would make things even more complicated than they were already.

'I think,' she told herself, 'that we shall have to go home soon.'

Equally she knew only too well that she really wanted to stay.

She had never enjoyed anything quite so much as staying in this fabulous Château with the Duc.

He paid her unbelievable compliments, there was no one to criticise or say unkind things.

'It is too good to last,' Lencia said to herself.

But she was smiling and her eyes were shining as she went into the drawing room, where the two men were waiting.

After dinner was over, they walked into the Music Room. It was decorated with flowers and was one of the prettiest rooms that Lencia had ever seen.

Seated at the piano, which was on a dais at the far end of the room, was a young man.

She had somehow expected an older musician or perhaps a woman to entertain them.

The young man seemed to be about the same age as Pierre.

He wore his hair rather too long, obviously as a sign of his artistic ability.

When he started to play the piano, Lencia knew that he was an outstanding musician.

He was now playing a dreamy waltz, one written by Richard Strauss, who had become popular not only in Europe but also in England.

"This is the moment I have been looking forward to," the Duc declared.

He put his arm around Lencia's waist.

As he took her hand in his, she felt a little thrill run through her.

She told herself that it was just because she was dancing with a handsome young man.

At the same time she was aware that it was the same feeling that she had felt last night when the Duc had touched her hand.

He then started to swing her around on the polished floor.

He was an excellent dancer, just as he excelled both as a horseman and a tennis player.

They danced in silence.

Yet there seemed to Lencia to be something magical about the music, the flower-scented room and, of course, the closeness of the Duc.

'It is because he is overwhelmingly delightful and such good company,' she told herself.

But she knew that what she was feeling was because she was so close to him.

His hand was holding hers and it was something very personal and very intimate.

They danced for a long time and the young man at the piano kept changing from tune to tune.

He always chose those that were romantic and dreamy.

The Duc finally stopped dancing at the open window.

They looked out into the garden where the great fountain was playing in the moonlight.

"I knew you would be as light as thistledown," the Duc said quietly, "and that we would move together as if we were one person. Did you feel that too?"

"You are a very good dancer," Lencia smiled.

"You have not answered my question," he replied.

She looked up at him and, when their eyes met, it was difficult for her to look away.

Then, as the music changed to a lively tune, the Duc drew her back into the room.

And once again they were moving round the floor.

He was right, they moved as if they were one person, joined not only by their bodies but by their minds.

It was not very late when the Duc thanked the pianist profusely and sent him away.

"I want to go on dancing," Alice complained.

"We have all had a long and somewhat arduous day and there will doubtless be another long one tomorrow," the Duc said, "so I think we should now retire to bed."

"I am sure you are right," Lencia said. "It is stupid to get overtired and nothing is more tiring than dramas."

She saw Alice shiver as she thought of the Comte and hurried her up to her room.

"It has been such a traumatic day," she said. "Go to sleep, dearest, and there is always tomorrow. Remember that the Duc has promised to take us to three different Château on the Loire."

"I am looking forward to seeing them all," Alice nodded.

She put her arms round her sister's neck and said,

"It is so lovely being here. I want to stay for ever and ever."

"It is no use, we shall soon have to go home," Lencia replied. "We cannot risk Papa and Stepmama arriving back and finding that we are missing."

Alice sighed.

"No, no, of course not. But how can we ever come here again if the Duc does not know where to find us?"

"Perhaps we will tell him and perhaps we will not," Lencia said. "I have not yet made up my mind."

Then she added quickly,

"Yes, I have! He must never, never know who we really are. You do understand?"

"I suppose so," Alice vaguely agreed, "but I want to see Pierre again."

"In a year or so it may be possible for you to meet him in London," Lencia suggested.

She knew that her sister was pouting and looking disappointed.

She kissed her goodnight and she went to her own room.

As she took off her mother's dress, she could hear the Duc saying,

"I have not seen you dressed like this before. You look so entrancing as a hundred men must have already told you."

Lencia shook her head and he countered,

"Where you live the men must be blind, deaf and dumb!"

"In England," Lencia said, "salmon, grouse and pheasants are so much more attractive."

The Duc laughed as she had intended him to do.

Then once again he was serious and he said,

"You bewilder me, but at the same time I am bewitched. What do you intend to do about it, Lencia?"

"What can I do?" she answered.

The Duc did not reply.

Alice and Pierre joined them and they were no longer having a private conversation.

'How can he say such things and not mean them?' Lencia asked herself as she undressed.

She brushed her hair vigorously as her mother had always told her to do.

She snuffed out the candles except for two beside her bed.

It was a very large bed hung with both muslin and satin curtains and it boasted a canopy of gilded cupids.

There were also cupids on the painted ceiling and surrounding the mirror on the dressing table.

'It is a room made for love,' Lencia thought to herself.

Then she blushed because it seemed to be the wrong thing for her to be thinking.

She said her prayers and, before putting out the last two candles, she looked around to have a last impression of the beautiful room that she knew she would never forget.

Then the door at the far end of the room opened. It led into a little boudoir, which she had hardly used because there had been no reason to do so.

She thought that it must be Alice for some reason coming to her.

Then, to her surprise, she saw that it was the Duc.

CHAPTER SIX

Lencia stared at the Duc in astonishment.

Then, as he crossed the room, she asked him,

"What has – happened? Why are you – here?"

"I have come to finish our conversation," the Duc replied gently.

"But you should not come into my bedroom," Lencia protested. "Please go – away."

The Duc smiled and, as he came nearer, he gazed at her.

He thought that he had not seen her look quite so lovely.

Her fair hair was falling over her shoulders and she was wearing one of her mother's diaphanous nightgowns that she had thought would impress the housemaids.

It revealed the curves of her breasts.

Then, as she saw the Duc looking at her, she pulled up the sheet to cover them.

"You must – go – away," she said sternly, but her voice trembled a little.

The Duc then sat down on the side of the bed.

"Now, listen, Lencia," he began. "You cannot go on mourning for a man whom you have admitted you did not really love. I think since you have been here that you and I have realised that we have so much in common that, if we are a little closer still, it would make us both very happy."

Lencia drew in her breath.

She knew exactly what he was saying to her.

She was shocked, but realised that it was her own fault.

"Please go – away," she repeated quickly, "and we will talk – about it – tomorrow."

"Why not now?" the Duc asked. "I want to tell you how lovely you are and how much I want you."

He paused for a moment and then he went on,

"Goodness knows I have been patient enough in respecting your bereavement. I believed rather foolishly that you had been very much in love with your husband."

It was difficult for Lencia to know how to reply to him.

She knew only that the Duc was sitting on her bed and looking at her.

He was wearing a long robe that was very much the same as her father wore.

Because she was frightened, not of him but of her feelings towards him, she said again,

"Please – please go away now and – perhaps we will think – about it."

"What have we to think about?" the Duc asked. "Except that you are the most beautiful woman I have ever seen in my life and I want you unbearably."

He gave a little smile before he added,

"I just cannot tell you how many hours I have lain awake at night, thinking about you and wanting to come here and tell you how irresistible I find you. But I thought that it right for me to wait."

"Of course – it is right," Lencia parried, "and please you must – go on – waiting."

"Why must I?" the Duc asked. "Tonight when we were dancing together and our steps matched each other's, I know, although you tried to hide it, that you were just as thrilled as I was."

He moved a little nearer to her and continued,

"Stop playing with me, Lencia, and let us be happy as the Gods have intended. We met by chance and found that they had in fact been very very kind to us."

He bent forward and Lencia thought that he was about to kiss her.

She gave a little cry and held him off with both hands.

"No! *No!*" she cried. "You are – not to touch me, you are – not to."

"Why?" the Duc asked. "You have bewildered me ever since I met you and still I find you impossible to understand."

He did not touch her, but his face was very near to hers as he went on,

"I think, although you will not admit it, that you want me just as I want you. Be sensible, Lencia, and let me teach you about love, a love that I am certain no Englishman could ever give you."

Lencia was still pushing at his chest with both her hands.

Now she spoke almost angrily,

"Go away – you are tempting me to do – something that is – wrong and that I – cannot do."

The Duc sat up, and her hands fell away from his chest.

"*Wrong?*" he demanded, "Why should it be wrong? You are free now and I am free. If we love each other, who is to find anything wrong in that?"

"I cannot – explain, but it would be wrong – very wrong and – wicked for me to – allow you to make – love to me."

"I don't understand."

"And I – cannot tell you – the reason," Lencia said. "Please be – kind, as you have – been so very – kind already and – go away and – forget me."

"Do you think that is possible?" the Duc exclaimed.

"It has to be for – reasons that I – cannot tell you."

There was a little sob in Lencia's voice.

Now there were tears in her eyes as she said,

"There is – nothing I can tell you – nothing I can say – except that you must – listen to me and please – leave me alone."

The Duc seemed to stiffen and then he replied,

"I have never forced myself on a woman who did not want me. If you really mean what you say, then there is nothing I can do, Lencia, but to leave you."

She did not reply and then after a moment he continued,

"Tell me this mysterious secret and then tell me exactly what you are hiding from me. You cannot leave me in ignorance and then expect me to understand you."

"I would tell you – if I – could," Lencia said. "But it is – impossible."

"Nothing is impossible," the Duc said. "We are two people attracted to each other, as was intended, I believe, from the beginning of time. As I have just said, I am a free man and you are a free woman, and what could be wrong in our love?"

He waited for a reply and, as she was silent, he carried on,

"Tell me, darling, tell me this momentous secret. If it is a problem that needs solving, I am quite certain that it is something I can happily do for you."

Now he was pleading with her it was even harder to resist him than it had been before.

She was seriously tempted to tell him the truth.

Then she knew that he might be shocked and, worse still, might think that it was a ruse to trap him into marriage.

If her father became aware that she was here unchaperoned, he would doubtless tell the Duc that he had ruined her reputation. And the only way he could make amends would be to offer her marriage.

It all flashed through Lencia's mind at once.

Then she said aloud,

"I would – tell you if it was – possible, but you must – believe me when I say – that it is absolutely – impossible. Therefore I can only – beg of you to be – kind and go away. Please let us forget that – this ever happened."

The Duc gave a deep sigh.

"Very well, Lencia," he said, "I have no wish to upset you or make you unhappy. But tomorrow perhaps you will change your mind."

The Duc rose to his feet.

As he did so, Lencia put out her hand towards him.

"Please don't be – angry," she begged. "You have made Alice and me so – happy here and we are – so grateful to you. I certainly don't – want to hurt you."

"This has never happened to me before," he said. "I feel frustrated at being confronted with a problem that I cannot solve and a mystery that I cannot penetrate."

"But you – are not – angry?" Lencia asked.

She looked up at him pleadingly, her eyes still glistening a little with tears.

He stood looking down at her and then unexpectedly he bent forward and kissed her.

It was a very gentle kiss.

As his lips touched hers, Lencia felt as if a shaft of sunshine swept through her whole body.

It was so rapturous and so incredible that she could hardly believe it was happening.

Just for a moment the Duc's kiss deepened.

Then he raised his head and sat very still gazing at her.

Then without a word he turned and left the room the way he had come without looking back.

It was only when he had gone that Lencia put her hands up to her face.

The rapture and ecstasy that she had felt from his kiss was still there.

Then, when she knew that she had lost him, the tears came and she hid her face in her pillow.

*

Lencia did not sleep until it was almost dawn.

Then she finally fell asleep from sheer exhaustion.

She kept turning over and over in her mind what the Duc had said to her and what she had said to the Duc.

But the end was always the same.

He had left her and the barrier between them was, she thought, even greater than it had been before.

'I love him,' she mused, '*of course I love him*. How could I have been with him all this time and not love everything he says and everything he does?'

Even as she confessed it to herself the temptation was still very present.

She wanted to listen to what he had suggested and to agree that they were made for each other, and let him love her as he wished to do.

It was then she knew that she must go home.

When the maid came to call her, she was deeply asleep.

As she drowsily opened her eyes, the maid said,

"Pardon, *madame*, there is a message here for you from Monsieur le Duc."

Lencia sat up in bed at once.

On the table there was an envelope addressed to Lady Winterton.

For a moment she just stared at it.

Was it possible, because he was angry with her that he was now asking her to leave his Château?

Had he no further interest in her as a guest after last night?

Her hands were trembling as she opened the envelope.

She then drew out the piece of writing paper inside. On it was written,

"*Beautiful Lencia,*

> *I have just received a message to say that the President of France stayed last night with one of my neighbours.*
>
> *He is very anxious to see Château Chaumont this morning and, of course, I have to show him round.*
>
> *It means unfortunately that Pierre, who has to go with me, and I will have to stay for luncheon. But we will hurry back to you as quickly as possible.*
>
> *I have, my lovely Goddess, something very important to discuss with you this evening.*

Yours,

Valaire."

Lencia read the letter through and then read it again slowly.

She knew, as if she was being told, that this was her ideal opportunity to leave without explanations, without arguments and without embarrassing farewells.

She climbed wearily out of bed and ran to her sister's room.

Alice was standing at the window in her nightgown looking out at the sunshine on the garden.

"It is a lovely day for riding," she smiled.

"Listen, Alice," Lencia said. "We have had an urgent message from home that we have to leave immediately."

Alice turned round sharply.

"From home?"

"That is what we shall tell the servants," Lencia said. "We have to leave and this is our opportunity to go without being questioned as to when the Duc or Pierre can meet us again."

As she spoke, she held out the note that the Duc had written to her and Alice read it.

"I really don't want to go," she said. "Surely we can stay here a few more days in this Paradise."

"If we do, it will not make it any easier to say 'goodbye'," Lencia insisted. "You will just have to think of this as a lovely dream and something sublime that we will always remember, which will never ever happen to us again."

"I want to see Pierre again," Alice protested in a sulky voice.

"Perhaps that can be arranged when you are a *debutante* and if he comes to London. But you know as well as I do that I cannot confess I am an imposter who has deceived the Duc into thinking I am a widow. And if Papa knew what we have done, he would be very very angry with us."

Alice gave a little shiver.

"Yes, of course, he would and you are right, Lencia. We had best go back home while we have the chance."

'Tell your maid to pack for you and I will tell mine. There is a train at eleven o'clock at Blois, which will take us to Paris and we can then catch the afternoon train to Calais."

"Oh, very well," Alice moaned, "but it seems to me awfully rude."

"Even ruder," Lencia replied, "when they ask us when they can see us again and we will not give them an address."

Alice must have seen the wisdom of this because she did not say anything more.

Lencia hurried back to her own bedroom.

The housekeeper was there and she expressed surprise that they had to leave in such a hurry.

As one of the maids started to pack Lencia's clothes, a message was sent to the stables to provide them with a carriage.

As was usual for the Duc's guests, another servant was sent to the Railway Station and he would notify the Stationmaster that they would require a private carriage.

As the Château was so beautifully run, there seemed to be no difficulties and everything was arranged smoothly.

Lencia tipped everyone generously and they seemed very grateful.

This she could well afford, not having had to pay a hotel bill while they were away.

She just had time to write a very short note to the Duc. She did not head it, but started off saying,

"I can only thank you from the bottom of my heart for all your kindness to me and my sister.
It has been a real joy being your guests and for

Alice having her dreams of Château Chaumont come true.

I amso sorry that we have to leave so hastily, but we have received word that we are required at home urgently.

This has been a magical moment that I shall never forget it for the rest of my life.
Lencia."

She put it into an envelope and addressed it to the Duc, knowing that he would receive it as soon as he returned.

As they drove down the drive, she looked back at the Château with an ache in her heart.

She felt that it would always be in her dreams, although she would never be able to see it again.

Alice was very quiet and hardly spoke until the train had left Blois Station.

They had a last glimpse of the trees that hid the river and then a fleeting sight of some Châteaux that they had not visited as they passed them by speedily.

"I shall never forget Pierre," Alice said, "but if he is not allowed to see me for at least a year, I suppose he will forget me."

"I am sure you will find a great many other young men to admire you," Lencia tried to comfort her a little.

"Do you think," Alice asked, "that you will be able to forget the Duc?"

It was a question that Lencia well knew the answer to. She had, however, no intention of sharing it with her sister.

"I said to him once," she replied, "that we were '*ships that pass in the night*' and that, dearest, is what we are. At the same time ships call at many different Ports, which I expect we shall do in our lives."

Alice did not answer, she was gazing out of the window at the passing countryside.

Lencia just knew by the expression on her face that she was miserable at leaving Pierre behind.

They crossed Paris and then found the train to Calais at the *Gare du Nord* without any difficulty.

At last Lencia felt that she could now relax.

In the carriage she sat with her feet up on the opposite seat and her eyes closed.

It was then that she allowed herself to think of the wonder and glory of the kiss that the Duc had given her last night.

She felt as if his lips were still pressed against hers and he could feel again the shaft of brilliant sunshine passing through her body.

The incredible rapture of it seemed to carry her up into the sky.

She had never been kissed before.

Yet she was wise enough to know that the kiss the Duc had given her was different not only from what she had expected but different from the kisses she would receive from other men.

'How could I be such a fool,' she asked herself, 'as to fall in love with a Frenchman? He has already loved a thousand women and will doubtless love a thousand more.'

Nevertheless, the wheels of the train kept on saying, '*I love – him, I love – him, I love – him,*' over and over again.

She felt the tears coming into her eyes and start to trickle down her cheeks.

She hastily wiped them away in case Alice should see them. Alice was, however, deep in her own thoughts.

Lencia could only pray and pray that her love for Pierre was not something that would spoil her life.

If Alice compared every other man she met in England with the fascinating Vicomte, she would be in the same boat as Lencia was.

Lencia remembered reading somewhere that one always pays for experience in life.

That, she thought, was what she was doing now.

She had been brave enough to take Alice to France in disguise and now she was paying the price because she had left her heart behind with a Frenchman.

To him she was just one more pretty 'flower' to be left by the wayside –

*

She found it hard later to remember anything about the journey.

It just seemed to be long hours of hearing the wheels of the train repeating, '*I love – you, I love – you.*'

It was a most uncomfortable Channel crossing with an extremely rough sea and a great number of the passengers were seasick.

Because it was unpleasant to be below, Lencia and Alice sat on deck.

They wrapped themselves in blankets that a Steward had kindly brought them. It was not particularly cold, but there was a very strong wind.

They sat in silence until they reached Dover.

Then there was the train journey back to London and a welcome from the surprised staff at Armeron House.

They had to explain that they had been staying with friends and, owing to an unexpected change of plans, they had to break their journey home in London.

"Now we have to go home," Lencia said, "and the quickest way would be by train."

"Papa always hates the train and drives whenever he can," Alice pointed out.

"It is enjoyable for him because he is driving his own horses," Lencia answered. "Those we have here in London can take us as far as *The Three Kings*, but I cannot see how we can go home from there except in a hired carriage."

"Oh! Let's go by train," Alice urged. "We shall be able to find a carriage of some sort to take us from the Station to Armeron Castle. After all it is only four miles."

Because she was feeling despondent, she did not care how they travelled as long as they reached home as quickly as possible.

They spent the night in London and the servants made them as comfortable as they could at short notice.

They made it very clear to Lencia that they did not like their new Mistress.

"We miss your Lady Mother, Miss Lencia," they said to her one after another. "We all loved her and things aren't the same now she's not here."

Lencia felt that it was something she could say herself.

It was just typical of her stepmother to upset the servants who had been with them for so many years.

"We're all lookin' forward, Miss Lencia," the housekeeper told her, "now you be out of mournin', to your comin' to London for parties and, of course, for your presentation to Her Majesty the Queen."

"I am afraid that has had to be postponed," Lencia said, "because her Ladyship is taking my place at the first Drawing Room."

She realised as she spoke how shocked the old housekeeper was at the idea. But it was some consolation to know that she too resented it.

Finally Lencia and Alice set off for the Railway Station.

The butler escorted them there and saw them safely into a locked carriage.

A large hamper of food had been prepared by the cook so that they 'need not eat that restaurant stuff'.

When they opened the hamper, Alice suggested,

"If we eat all this, we shall be too fat to get out through the door."

"The servants in London love us, if no one else does," Lencia said. "I think in a way they are making more fuss over us just to spite Stepmama."

"They hate her just as I do," Alice said. "It is agony to think that we have to put up with her all through the summer."

Then she looked at her sister and laughed.

"It is a good thing that she could not see you the other night in Mama's beautiful dress dancing with a Duc. She would have wanted to tear your eyes out!"

"Oh, do be careful, Alice," Lencia said. "No one must ever know that has happened and, if we talk about it even just together, we might be overheard."

"Well, I want to talk about the wonderful time we had in France," Alice protested. "I want to dance with Pierre and race him up the stairs. Instead of which I will have to listen to Stepmama telling me what a success she has been in Sweden."

"As soon as we get back, we will ride the horses and forget her," Lencia proposed.

It was, however, more easily said than done.

When she went riding the next morning with Alice, she kept remembering what fun it had been riding out with the Duc by her side.

She remembered all the flattering compliments that he had been kind enough to pay her.

Of course, even to think of him brought back the unbelievable wonder of his kiss.

It was impossible for her not to think that very soon he would be kissing someone else in the same way.

'How can I ever love anyone else, having loved him?' Lencia asked herself angrily when she was lying in bed that night trying to go to sleep.

In the darkness she felt that she could see him all too clearly sitting on the side of her bed and pleading with her.

'Why did I say 'no'? Why did I run away?' she asked herself again and again.

She knew all the answers, but the questions were still there in her heart.

Nothing seemed to erase them from her consciousness.

The second day after they came home they learned that the Earl and their Stepmama had arrived back in London from Sweden.

"They are coming down here this afternoon," Lencia said. "Mr. Bentley has instructions to send the carriage to the Station for them."

"What are we going to say if Papa does find out, as he is bound to, that we have been to London in his absence?" Alice asked nervously.

"We went up to London because I had to go to the dentist," Lencia said. "You know that we have always been to the same dentist and Papa would not dream of having anyone else treat us."

"Then what happened?" Alice asked.

"Then we went to stay with a schoolfriend of mine whom I will invent or else use the name of one I have mentioned in a letter when I have written home to Mama and Papa."

"So we stayed in London," Alice questioned, trying to make it all clear in her mind.

"We stayed in London with my friend, my teeth were treated by the dentist and then we came home."

"I will try not to forget it," Alice said, "but it will be very difficult not to tell Papa what he missed by not going to France with us."

She was only teasing, but Lencia scolded her,

"For Heaven's sake, Alice, we have managed to escape without anyone penetrating our disguise and we must not push our luck too far. You know how angry Papa would be."

"Egged on by Stepmama," Alice agreed bitterly, "who would be delighted if we were in trouble."

"Well, don't give her the satisfaction of having a genuine cause for complaint," Lencia emphasised.

She had thought their stay away through very carefully and she was very certain that her father would not be suspicious if she and Alice told the same tale.

When the Earl finally arrived home, she realised that she need not have worried.

Their father was looking rather tired and seemed not to have enjoyed himself in Sweden all that much.

But their stepmother never stopped talking about it.

She told them how they had been received almost as if they were Royalty, describing in detail the palatial rooms they were given and the huge dinner parties that they had attended.

She went on to describe the ball, the presents the Prince had received and the speeches that had been made.

It all took a good long time and Lencia forced herself to sit looking attentive, as if she was really interested in what her stepmother was saying at length.

"We promised to go back again next year," the Countess trilled triumphantly, "and we have also been invited to visit Denmark. That is something I know we shall hugely enjoy."

"What about you, Papa?" Lencia asked him.

She realised that her father had not said a word for at least twenty minutes.

"I find it rather tiring to go gadding about when I want to be at home," he replied. "Tell me about the horses."

Lencia described how well they all were.

Fortunately he did not ask if she had been riding every day but took it for granted.

It did come up a little later that Lencia had had to go to London to see the dentist.

But almost before she could say anything, the Countess interrupted by interposing,

"That reminds me, I want my bedroom in London redecorated and the sooner it is done the better."

The Earl looked surprised.

"What is wrong with it, my dear?" he asked. "It always seemed delightful to me."

"You are so understanding, dearest," his wife replied, "so you will, I know, appreciate that I want my bedroom to represent me and me alone."

She put out her hand to touch his shoulder as she added,

"Of course I want to look beautiful in it for you. And who is a better judge of beauty than the handsome and very clever Earl of Armeron?"

She was flattering him again, Lencia knew and, because it was false and insincere, it made her feel sick.

She stood up from her chair and then walked across the room.

"I meant to tell you, Lencia," her father said as if he had suddenly thought of it, "that I saw the Lord Chamberlain about your presentation. He has managed to squeeze you into the last one, which will take place in June."

"Oh, very well, Papa," Lencia said, "but I would much rather have been in one earlier."

"The Lord Chamberlain said it was impossible," the Earl replied, "and I am very sorry that we had to change it from the first."

"Perhaps it would be much better, dearest, if Lencia waited another year," the Countess murmured.

"No, of course not," the Earl replied. "Lencia is now all of nineteen. She should have been presented last year if she had not been in mourning."

"I expect she would feel rather out of place with all those young *debutantes* of seventeen and eighteen," the Countess said. "But I daresay that no one will really notice that she is any older."

Lencia knew that she was trying hard to make it all difficult for her.

She thought, however, that it was best not to reply or make any objections.

"What we must have," the Earl suggested quickly, "is some young parties for Lencia in London and perhaps it would be wise to give our ball rather sooner than we intended so that we will be invited to all the other subsequent balls and parties."

"I am looking forward to a ball," the Countess proposed. "But we don't want too many young people. *Debutantes* are always rather heavy on hand and you know, my dearest, I want to shine as a hostess just because I am your wife."

Lencia thought that if the ball did ever take place, the number of young girls would be reduced to a very bare minimum.

When they had gone out of the room, Alice said,

"She is determined to eclipse you and I am not certain what we can do about it."

"There is nothing we can do," Lencia answered. "She dislikes us both and is determined that we shall have as little attention as possible not only from Papa but from everyone else."

"I hate her," Alice said. "If she goes on like this, I shall go back to France and beg the Duc to take me into his Château."

"Oh, Alice, do be careful!" Lencia warned her. "When you do say things like that, I am always afraid someone is listening at the door and will tell Papa. Just think what a weapon against us the whole story would be in Stepmama's hands."

"That is true," Alice admitted. "Think what would happen to me. I would be locked in the schoolroom here in the country. As it is I doubt if I will be allowed to put a single foot in Armeron House. She will be entertaining all the smart people who do not like young girls like us."

She spoke so bitterly that Lencia put her arms around her.

"Don't be unhappy, dearest," she said, "I feel that everything will come right in the end. I don't know how yet, but I just know."

"I hope you are right," Alice said. "Home is not — like home anymore without — Mama."

Her voice broke on the last words.

Lencia could only hold her tight and kiss her.

"You will have to be brave," she said, "and we will fight this together. We must not let Stepmama get us down. That would be a victory for her."

"Yes, of course it would," Alice agreed at once, "and if Pierre was here, I know he would rescue me."

"I am sure he would," Lencia nodded. "But just think of the commotion if he suddenly appeared saying what a lovely time — we all had together in France."

Alice laughed.

"I would just like to see Stepmama's face! But she would be impressed with him because he is a Vicomte."

"Perhaps somehow when we go to London you can become acquainted with him. He did say he often comes here."

"I shall certainly try," Alice said, "and I promise you, dearest sister, that I will be very careful."

"You had better be or Stepmama will shut us up here in the dungeon and we will never see daylight again!"

They both laughed at this.

But, when Lencia went to bed that night, she was still worrying about Alice.

She thought that she must arrange to have a long talk with her father.

She would suggest that if she was going to be presented at the last Drawing Room, Alice should be too.

Lots of girls were presented at the age of seventeen and Alice would actually be eighteen just before Christmas.

'Why on earth did I not think of it before?' Lencia asked herself. 'Then Alice can make some friends of her own age and go to parties that we hope will not include Stepmama.'

She went to sleep thinking about Alice and then inevitably she dreamt of the Duc.

*

The next day the Countess seemed to be determined to antagonise everyone she came in contact with except, of course, for the Earl.

She was very disagreeable to the housekeeper about the condition of some of the rooms and she told the cook that the food disgusted her because it was so English.

She informed the old butler that the footmen were sloppy and a disgrace.

Lencia felt as if the whole house was vibrating against her.

'There was always a lovely atmosphere when Mama was here,' she thought. 'How can Stepmama upset everyone and everything quite so soon and so easily?'

Her father wanted them to go riding with him.

The Countess, however, insisted that he should take her driving round the estate as she had seen so little of it.

The girls went riding alone and because they were both somewhat depressed, they did not talk to each other.

They jumped the low hedges and galloped fast over the flat ground.

When they came back to The Castle, Alice commented sourly,

"This is the first time in my life it has made me shudder to enter my own home. It used to be such a happy place."

"I know," Lencia said. "But I don't think that Stepmama will stay here for very long. She will find it too dull. And when she and Papa go to London, perhaps we can have some friends to stay."

"Whom shall we ask?" Alice queried. "Whom do we really want to be with?"

They both knew the answer to that.

Lencia never seemed to have a chance to talk to her father alone.

However, the opportunity actually came after tea.

The Countess announced that she thought English tea was a waste of time and perhaps they would like to dispense with it.

Both Lencia and Alice said quickly,

"No! Of course not"

To their relief, their father agreed with them,

"I think it would be a great mistake. If there is one thing I dislike, it is breaking traditions that have been carried on for generations."

Their stepmother acquiesced immediately.

"Of course, dearest," she said, "you are quite right. It was very stupid of me to suggest such a thing. I was only thinking of saving the servants. But that again is unnecessary, as you wisely, because you are so clever, have pointed out."

She rose to her feet as she finished speaking, kissed the Earl on the cheek and said,

"I am going to lie down before dinner, because I hope to look beautiful and to entertain you by being witty."

"You are always witty," the Earl declared.

"But not as witty as you," his wife replied. "Someone in Sweden said to me that they had never known an Englishman as such fun as you are."

The Earl looked pleased and the Countess moved towards the door.

"Don't be late for dinner, girls," she said severely. "You know how your father hates to be kept waiting, bless his heart."

As she left the room, Alice and Lencia looked at each other.

The Earl made himself more comfortable in his armchair.

"Now, Papa, we want to talk to you," Lencia began, "and start making plans."

"Yes, of course," the Earl agreed. "We have not had a chance to talk about things until now."

Lencia sat down on one side of him while Alice sat on the hearth rug at his feet.

"This is just like old times," the Earl smiled. "You know, my dearest girls, I love you both very much and want to do whatever will make you happy."

"I knew you would say that, Papa," Lencia commented as she smiled back at him.

"I must admit," he went on, "I felt guilty when I went off to Sweden knowing how much Alice particularly wanted to see the Loire Châteaux. But I am sure that it is something we can manage next year, if not before."

He sounded somewhat doubtful.

Lencia was very certain that if he did suggest anything like that, their stepmother would inevitably prevent it.

"Now what I want to say to you, Papa is – " she was about to resume.

At that moment the door opened.

"Monsieur le Duc de Montrichard, my Lord," the butler announced.

CHAPTER SEVEN

For a moment everyone seemed to be frozen with surprise.

Then the Earl jumped up, saying,

"Valaire, my dear boy, I had no idea that you were in London."

The Earl walked briskly across the room to shake his hand and saying,

"I am delighted to see you and it is far too long since you came here."

"I have come for your help," the Duc replied.

As he was speaking, he suddenly saw Lencia for the first time.

As their eyes met, she put her finger quickly to her lips.

"My help?" the Earl repeated. "But, of course, you know that I will help you in any way that I possibly can."

He turned round and added,

"Come and meet my family."

They walked towards Lencia and Alice.

They were standing and feeling as if their hearts were beating far too quickly for them to breathe.

"Now, this is Lencia," the Earl said as he reached her. "I think the last time you were here you were ten years old and Lencia must have been one, so you can hardly be expected to recognise each other."

"No, of course not," the Duc agreed, "it was a long time ago."

"And this is Alice," the Earl went on. "If she was born when you were last here with your father, she would have been just in the cradle."

As the Duc stepped forward to shake her hand, he felt Lencia pressing his fingers as if she was warning him.

The Earl then continued,

"Now, can I offer you some refreshment? I suppose you have come down from London."

"No, thank you, I want nothing except to talk to you, my Lord," the Duc replied.

"Where are you staying?" the Earl questioned.

There was a little pause.

Then with a smile that Lencia thought was irresistible, the Duc said,

"I was hoping for old time's sake that I might stay with you here in Armeron Castle."

"But, of course, my dear boy!" the Earl exclaimed. "Naturally we are really delighted to welcome you here."

"You must forgive me for not notifying you before I came," the Duc said, "but I made up my mind only at the very last moment to come to England."

The Earl sat down in the chair he had been sitting in before and the Duc sat next to him.

"Now tell me how I can help you."

Lencia held her breath.

She was aware that the Duc was thinking frantically what he should say to her father.

"I seem to remember," he began slowly, "that your father kept a diary, as did my father. There is an author at the moment who is eager to write his biography. I wondered if in your father's diary there would be mention of the times my father came here and what happened on those occasions."

"A biography! What a splendid idea!" the Earl exclaimed. "And, of course, your father was a very distinguished man. I have kept all of my father's diaries and they are in a special room upstairs. I will show them to you."

The Earl rose to his feet and turned to Lencia,

"You girls take the Duc to the Tower Room while I tell the servants to arrange for his luggage to be taken upstairs and to notify your stepmother that he is here."

"Yes, Papa," Lencia said meekly.

They all walked towards the door.

When they reached the hall, Lencia, the Duc and Alice went upstairs leaving the Earl talking to the butler.

Only when she was sure that her father would not notice, Lencia moved quicker.

They hurried down the passage to the room that contained the relics of their grandfather.

As they reached it, Lencia said to Alice in a whisper,

"Keep guard."

She and the Duc went inside and, before she could speak, he said,

"I have to see you alone, you realise that?"

"Yes, of course," Lencia answered. "But please be very careful, Papa does not know we went to France and he would be very angry if he finds out."

"I guessed that when I saw your face and you put your finger up to your lips," the Duc said. "When can I talk to you?"

"When everyone else has gone to bed," Lencia said in a low voice. "Go to the end of this passage where you will find another staircase. At the bottom there is a door into the garden."

She ran across to the window and the Duc followed her.

"You see the fountain," she said. "If you look to the left of it, you will see there is a gate, which leads into the Herb Garden. No one will see us in there. Papa's windows look out onto the other side."

She had hardly finished what she was saying when Alice called out from the door,

"Papa is coming!"

Lencia turned towards the bookcase.

"Here are the diaries," she said, "and, as you can see, there are a great number of them."

The Earl came into the room.

"It will take you some time, Valaire," he said, "to find what you are seeking. But if you were ten when you came here last, that is seventeen years ago, which will make it 1878."

"Of course, of course," the Duc agreed. "But my father stayed with yours I think quite a number of times before that."

"He did and we will just have to look and see what we can find," the Earl suggested.

Watching them Lencia felt almost faint at the shock of seeing the Duc so unexpectedly.

At the same time she was aware that her heart had turned a complete somersault.

It was difficult to think of anything except that he was there.

She could see him again and hear him after the hours she had lain awake in her thinking of him and missing him so much.

Only when they went to dress for dinner did Alice come into her room and say,

"I must know where Pierre is."

"We will find out before the Duc leaves," Lencia said, "but we must be very careful."

"I nearly gave a loud scream when he was announced," Alice said. "I thought I must be dreaming."

"I thought so too," Lencia replied.

At dinner she found it almost impossible to eat anything with the Duc sitting on the other side of the table talking to her stepmother.

Or rather the Countess was talking to him.

She was absolutely delighted to have the Duc of Montrichard in The Castle.

She came down to dinner covered in jewels and determined, Lencia sensed, to make an impression on him.

"I have heard so much about you, *monsieur*," she said in what she thought was her most fascinating voice. "My friends in Paris spoke of you so often."

She gave him a provocative glance from under her mascaraed eyelashes and went on,

"Of course they told me how many hearts you have broken and what a fantastic success you are."

"You must not believe all you hear," the Duc cautioned her.

"But I want to believe it!" the Countess said. "And I can assure you that you look exactly as I expected you to, so very handsome and *un vrai galant*."

She continued during the meal to flatter the Duc extravagantly. It was the same way that she flattered her husband.

Listening to her stepmother, Lencia wondered if this was the sort of thing that the Duc enjoyed.

If so, Lencia felt that he could not really have enjoyed being with her in the way he said he had.

By the time dinner had finished she realised suddenly that she and Alice had said nothing throughout the meal.

She was quite sure that it was exactly what her stepmother had intended from the start of dinner.

When they moved into the drawing room, the Countess sat beside the Duc on the sofa.

She continued to talk of Paris and of the success he was with her friends.

"You may have a reputation," she said, "of being a very naughty boy but who can blame you for that?"

"Who indeed?" the Duc responded.

He was looking towards Lencia as he spoke.

She found it an agony to hear her stepmother talking on and on about his successes with other women.

She finally told her father that she was feeling tired.

She and Alice slipped away without saying 'goodnight' to their stepmother or to the Duc.

"You see just how she goes on," Alice said when they were outside the door. "If we had a dinner party for our friends, I don't suppose that we should be able to say a word to them."

"Not if they were handsome and of any importance," Lencia said bitterly.

She went up to her room and stood waiting by the window.

It seemed that a century passed before at last she saw the Duc walk across the lawn and past the fountain.

He found the gate she had told him about that led into the Herb Garden and disappeared inside.

It was then that she ran down the stairs and hurriedly followed him into the garden.

Her father and stepmother's windows, as she had told him, looked out on the other side of The Castle.

So there was no one to see her run across the garden.

It was a bright moonlit night and countless stars filled the sky.

They glittered on the smaller fountain that was playing in the centre of the Herb Garden.

It made, she thought, an appropriate frame for the Duc, who was standing with his back to it.

Now, having run across the lawn, she was moving more slowly.

When she reached him, for a moment it seemed as if both of them were stricken into a silence.

Then at last in a voice that did not sound at all like her own, Lencia asked him,

"Why – did you – come here?"

"How could you have gone away without telling me? How could you have left me in that cruel manner?" the Duc asked. "I was just frantic when I thought that I would never see you again."

"I – had to – go."

"Why?" the Duc demanded.

Because she did not want to answer this question, she stammered quickly,

"What made – you come – here of all – places?"

He smiled and somehow it broke the tension a little.

"Alice left one of her books behind. It was, of course, about the Châteaux of the Loire and inside was the book-plate of Armeron Castle."

Lencia gave a little exclamation.

"It belongs to the library here."

"That is what I thought," the Duc replied, "so I came to England at once to ask the Earl of Armeron if he had any knowledge of a Lady Winterton living in this neighbourhood."

"So that is how it happened," Lencia cried.

"How could you have done anything so dangerous as to go alone with Alice to France?"

"When Papa, who had previously promised to take us, went instead to Sweden with our stepmother," Lencia explained, "she was so very disappointed. And I did not – think it would be – dangerous if I pretended to be – a married woman."

"Looking like you do, surely you must have realised that there are many men in France who would find you irresistible. Myself for instance."

Lencia said nothing and after a moment he asked,

"Why did you go away so impetuously without even saying 'goodbye'?"

Still Lencia did not speak and so he carried on,

"Were you not at all curious when I said that I had something to discuss with you after I returned home that day?"

"I knew – what that – would be," Lencia said in a very low voice, "and – I was afraid I – might say 'yes'."

The Duc stared at her for a short moment and then he said,

"What I was going to ask you, my darling, was if you would do me the very great honour of becoming my wife?"

Lencia gave a gasp and looked up at him.

"You were – going to – ask me to – marry you?"

"As I am asking you now."

"But you – said after – what had – happened to you – you would – never marry again."

"That was before I found you," he smiled.

He put out his hands and laid them on her shoulders, touching her for the first time.

"Now, listen to me," he said. "I knew from the very first moment I saw you not only that you are the most beautiful woman who I had ever seen but as well that, in a way I could not explain, you belonged to me. Because of what I went through as a young man, I had been very determined to keep my freedom."

Lencia made a little movement, but he did not release her and went on,

"But when I saw you holding that small baby in your arms, I knew that I wanted you as my wife and the mother of my children."

Lencia looked at him in surprise and he then added,

"But I was still fighting against what my heart and my soul told me and that was why I came to your bedroom."

"Yet after – that, when I – sent you away – you wanted to – marry me?" Lencia asked.

"I was always suspicious that you were not what you were pretending to be," the Duc answered. "You seemed in so many ways so young and so innocent and, although it did seem incredible, untouched."

Lencia blushed.

"You really – thought – that?"

"I thought it," the Duc replied. "Then, when I kissed you, I knew two things. First that you had never been kissed before and secondly that you belonged to me completely and absolutely."

His voice deepened as he continued,

"I have never, and this is the truth Lencia, felt so moved by a kiss, which was different and delicate from anything I had ever known."

"Is that – really – true?" she whispered.

"I think perhaps we should prove it," the Duc suggested with a twinkle in his eyes.

He pulled her close against him and kissed her at first very gently and then much more possessively.

It seemed to Lencia as if they were somehow a part of the fountain.

They were being thrown higher and higher up towards the stars until they could actually touch them.

Only when the ecstasy that the Duc aroused in her seemed almost unbearable, because it was so utterly and totally wonderful, did he raise his head.

"Now you understand," he said in a deep voice. "Neither of us can fight against that. You are mine, Lencia, and I am yours, as God made us to be and He had always intended that we should be together again in this life."

"I – love – you," Lencia whispered. "I love – you – I love you for what – seems to have been a very long time. But I – never thought that you would – really love me."

"I know exactly what you thought," the Duc said, "but, my precious, neither of us can deny that what we are feeling now is so perfect that it can have only come from Heaven."

"That is – what I am – thinking," Lencia murmured.

"We think the same, we *are* the same, we are one person," the Duc said. "The question now is quite simple, how soon will you marry me, my darling Lencia?"

"As soon as – you want me to," Lencia said and hid her face against his shoulder.

"That is now, this moment," the Duc answered. "But, my precious one, I have something else to ask you, although you may think it a little strange."

Lencia raised her head.

"What is – it?" she enquired rather nervously.

"I want you to be very brave and run away with me," he replied.

Lencia stared at him.

"Why?" she asked.

The Duc's arms tightened for a moment around her and then he said,

"What we are feeling now is so perfect and so wonderful, I could not bear it to be spoilt."

"Nor – could – I," Lencia stammered.

"If we have a grand Wedding such as everyone will expect," the Duc went on, "we shall have to wait for a month, perhaps more. During that time I know only too well that everyone will tell you stories about me."

He drew in his breath as he continued,

"They may be true, but I do *not* want you to hear them. Even if you try not to listen, they will insist on talking of how many women there have been in my life and a number of other things that I would much rather you did not know."

His voice strengthened as he said finally,

"They are past, they are finished with, they have no place in our future together."

Lencia understood exactly what he was saying.

She remembered how her stepmother had kept referring to the love affairs he had had in France with her various friends and the way she called him 'a naughty boy' and at the same time revelled in his naughtiness.

Lencia could appreciate how it would make everything seem rather cheap and tawdry and it would undoubtedly frighten her when she thought about the future.

The Duc was following her thoughts and he then said,

"Exactly! That is why, my darling, I want you to be brave enough to come away with me immediately. Nothing and nobody must spoil this wonder and ecstasy and that we have been so lucky to have found together."

His voice was very tender as he went on,

"How you can make me feel like this I don't understand myself. I not only want you as I have never wanted a woman before but it makes me worship you because you are perfection itself."

"How can you say things like – that to – me?" Lencia asked. "At the – same time it is what I – want you to – feel if it makes you happy."

"I am happier at this moment than I have ever been in my whole life," the Duc answered. "And I know now that when they called me Monsieur Mille-Feuilles, what I was seeking was a wife who loves me and a beautiful home where we can love our children together."

It flashed through Lencia's mind that he would be as kind and sweet to his children as he had been to the woodcutter's little boy when he had hurt his knee.

She moved a little closer to him and said in a whisper,

"I will – run away with – you, but you – must tell me – what to do."

"My precious, my sublime, that is what I wanted you to say to me," the Duc exclaimed.

Then he was kissing her again, not only her lips but her eyes, her little straight nose and the softness of her neck.

It gave her strange feelings that she had never known.

"I have so much to teach you," he said as he felt her quiver. "And love, my darling one, can be a very long but fabulous lesson."

"I love – you – I love – you," Lencia sighed. "But just how can we – run away without everyone trying to – stop me?"

"That is exactly what they will do unless we are very clever about it."

He kissed her forehead before he added,

"When you left me, I was determined, if I ever did find you, that somehow I would take you away with me. Now it will be much easier than I thought it would be."

"But how! *How!*" Lencia asked.

"Today is Tuesday," the Duc declared. "If I leave tomorrow, can you get to London on Thursday?"

"Yes, I can say I am going to – the dentist again," Lencia smiled a secretive smile.

"Then I will collect you from Armeron House at eleven o'clock on Friday morning. We will be married and then we will disappear until all the commotion and chatter about us has been forgotten."

"It sounds too – wonderful," Lencia said, "but we will have to be – very careful that – no one guesses what we are doing."

"You must be very careful," the Duc cautioned. "Tell Alice, but no one else, and swear her to secrecy."

With an effort, Lencia remembered that Alice wanted to know about Pierre and she said a little tentatively,

"Where is – Pierre?"

"He is in Hampshire, looking for Alice, where she told him she lived."

"And he wanted to – find her?" Lencia enquired.

"He is very much in love with her," the Duc replied.

"How wonderful," Lencia exclaimed, "because Alice loves him! But how are we to get them together without Papa being suspicious in any way?"

The Duc smiled.

"That is quite easy. Before I leave I will ask your father if he would be kind enough to let my nephew see his horses. I know from what you told me that he has some excellent ones. And so if Pierre comes as a guest to The Castle, who would be surprised if they fall in love with each other at first sight?"

Lencia laughed.

"Oh, you are *so* clever! That is exactly what could happen without anyone thinking it at all strange."

"I will be honest with you," the Duc said, his eyes twinkling, "My sister and her husband were thinking of arranging a marriage for Pierre and they would not have been prepared to accept Miss Alice Austin. Lady

Alice Leigh of Armeron Castle is a very different matter!"

Lencia laughed and then she suggested,

"Please, darling, arrange it. I want Alice to be happy and she will never be happy living with our stepmother."

"I thought that myself at dinner last night and that is yet another reason why I want you to come away with me as quickly as possible."

Lencia knew that he did not want her to believe the stories her stepmother would tell her about him.

Very stiffly she next said,

"You know I think you are – wonderful. Even if I have only two or three years of – perfect happiness with you, it will be – better than – a lifetime of – misery because I – refused you."

"I would not allow you to refuse me," the Duc asserted. "And on our sixtieth Wedding Anniversary or perhaps it will be our eightieth, you shall tell me what a wonderful husband I have been and you have never had a moment's worry about me."

Lencia chuckled.

"Perhaps that is just asking too much. But as long as you love me and as long as we are together, I shall feel as if – I am living in Heaven."

Because she spoke so sincerely to him, the Duc could only kiss her until they were both breathless.

Then he stated,

"I must send you to bed, my darling. You have so much to do and to think about before Friday."

"I am – afraid," Lencia said, "I will not have a very elaborate trousseau."

The Duc smiled.

"I am a Frenchman and I cannot imagine anything I shall enjoy more than dressing you as only a Frenchman can to make you even more beautiful than you are at the moment."

"I shall – enjoy that," Lencia murmured.

He kissed her again before he urged,

"Go to bed, my darling, and dream of me."

'That is what I have done ever since we left you," Lencia said. "Then, because I thought I would never see – you again, I have – cried."

"I will never allow you to cry in the future," the Duc said. "But if you cried, can you imagine how I felt when I had no idea where I could begin to look for you, except that you had vaguely told me that you lived in Kent."

"Then the servants brought you the book," Lencia said. "It was very careless of Alice to leave it behind."

"It had slipped down the side of the bed," the Duc explained, "and I suppose because Alice was packing in a hurry she did not notice that it was missing."

"But it brought you here and how very grateful I am that Alice had a passion for seeing the Châteaux of the Loire."

"Now you will live in one and so will she," the Duc said. "God moves in a mysterious way and we can thank Him on our knees that His way has been our way."

He kissed her again and then he said,

"You are quite certain, my precious one, that you do not mind being married secretly and with a rather short Service as I am a Roman Catholic and you are not."

There was a little pause and then Lencia answered him,

"I have not thought about it for a long time, but actually I was Baptised a Catholic."

"How is that possible?" the Duc asked in astonishment.

"I expect my father told your father, but you did not hear of it," Lencia said. "I was born in France. Papa was sent on a special mission to Paris when Mama was expecting me and had reached her seventh month. He wanted to go without her, but she said jokingly that she would not trust him with all those beautiful French ladies – and I think it was very sensible of her."

The Duc's eyes twisted because he knew that she was thinking of his reputation.

He did not speak and Lencia went on,

"While they were driving outside Paris, they had a slight carriage accident. It was not a serious one, but Mama realised that I had started to arrive too soon."

"What did your father do?" the Duc asked.

"Papa took her into a Convent at St. Clois where the nuns looked after Mama very well and brought me into the world. Because I was so very small and they thought I might die, I was Baptised by their Priest."

She smiled and moved a little closer to the Duc, saying,

"I think I was born for you, so I lived. Of course, when we came back to England, I was Baptised again with the usual English collection of Godfathers and Godmothers."

"But you were first Baptised a Catholic," the Duc said. "That makes things much easier."

"And, of course," Lencia said softly, "when we are – married I would like to – become a Roman Catholic so that we can go – to Church together."

"With our children," the Duc added, "that is what I hoped and prayed you would say. As you must realise, my precious one, that will make my home just as perfect as I want it to be."

They moved across the Herb Garden.

When they reached the gate, the Duc kissed her passionately for a long time.

Then, as if everything was settled between them, they walked back to The Castle hand in hand.

Only when she was alone in her bed did Lencia say over and over again,

'Thank You, God – thank You for giving him to me.'

*

The following morning the Duc left early.

Lencia began to sort out what clothes she would take with her to London.

She really had very few new dresses and they were certainly not ones she thought good enough for her Wedding.

There might not be anyone present, but she wanted to look beautiful for the Duc.

She wanted him always to remember their Marriage Ceremony, however quiet it might be.

When she told Alice what was happening, her sister was in a wild state of excitement, especially when she learned that she would be able to see Pierre again.

"Don't look so excited at going to London," Lencia warned her, "otherwise Stepmama may suspect that something is up! The dentist could certainly not bring such a shine to your eyes."

"I love him, Lencia," Alice confessed, "and if he really does love me, could anything be more marvellous?"

The Earl suggested that he might go with them, but their stepmother stopped that idea immediately.

She said she intended to be at Armeron House the following week and the girls could then stay at The Castle.

She said that she could see no point in everyone moving just before the weekend.

"I think it will have to be the week after that," the Earl replied, "because the Duc was telling me that his nephew, the Vicomte Bethune, is eager to see my horses. I have suggested that he comes to stay this next Saturday for at least a week."

"The Vicomte Bethune?" the Countess said. "I should most certainly like to meet him. I believe he is a very good-looking young man."

"All their family are," the Earl said in a lofty way. "And when he leaves then, of course, my dear, if you want to go to London, we will open the house."

"I will give several parties," the Countess proposed.

The Earl nodded his approval with a slight hesitation.

But Lencia was aware that her stepmother gave her a hard look as if to say that she had no intention of including her in her parties.

'Fortunately,' Lencia thought, 'she does not know that I shall be having the most perfect party of all on my own.'

She was well aware that her stepmother would be furious and intensely jealous when she learnt that she had married a Duc.

She would also feel defrauded that she had not been able to have a grand Wedding.

If she was not the bride, she would at least have been the hostess!

'Valaire is so right in thinking that there is no need for all that,' Lencia said to herself as she concentrated on her packing.

She took with her some very pretty nightgowns that had belonged to her mother, also a lace-trimmed chiffon *negligée,* which she hoped that the Duc would find entrancing.

There was no point in including the gowns, except for the one she had worn for dinner at his Château as they would make her look too old.

However, she had one plan that she thought was very important.

She and Alice travelled to London on the early train on Thursday morning and they were accompanied by one of the older housemaids to look after them.

A carriage from Armeron House had been ordered to meet them at Victoria Station.

When they had stepped into it, Lencia told the footman that she wished to drive to Bond Street.

She gave him the address of a shop where her mother had always bought her clothes and she had visited it with her several times.

When Lencia explained who she was, she was greeted warmly.

She said that she wanted a very beautiful white dress to wear for a very special occasion.

The white afternoon dresses were, however, she thought, rather unattractive and they did not have the softness that she somehow felt was essential.

A *vendeuse* then produced an evening gown of white chiffon that was exactly what she wanted except for the bodice.

The woman, however, promised that by the evening she could fill in the neck and add sleeves to the gown.

This, Lencia well knew, would make a really lovely Wedding dress for the Duc to see her wearing as they made their vows.

Because it clung to her figure and was a very soft material, she hoped it would remind him of the Goddess he thought her to be.

She also found two pretty day dresses that suited her. They were in pale colours, which she hoped made her look like a flower.

She knew, as they were being married secretly, that she could not wear a veil or a tiara at her Wedding.

However she found a hat that was really little more than a wreath of flowers. It had just a surround of transparent material that made it somehow look like a halo.

"You look wonderful in that hat," Alice whispered and Lencia hoped that she was right.

They did not get to Armeron House until after teatime and the servants were wondering what had happened to them.

"We had to do a large amount of shopping," Lencia explained.

"We thought perhaps you'd had an accident, my Lady," the butler said and was looking worried.

"No, I am quite safe," Lencia replied to him.

She and Alice had a quiet supper together and then went to bed early.

It was impossible for Lencia to sleep because she was so excited.

At the same time she knew that, however angry her father might be at the letter that she had written to him, she was doing the right thing.

As Alice had so often said,

"Home is not home without Mama."

It would, in fact, Lencia reflected, be far better for her father if they were not there to irritate their stepmother.

When morning came, the sun was shining brightly through her bedroom window.

Lencia rose early so as to allow herself plenty of time to make herself look beautiful for the Duc.

Alice came running up the stairs to tell her that he had arrived.

She went down feeling a little nervous because at that moment she was stepping out of her old world and into a new one, a world that she knew she had very little knowledge about.

But the Duc was the only one that mattered in this new firmament of hers.

He was looking extremely handsome, wearing evening dress that was correct in France,.

His orders and decorations were on the breast of his evening coat, while the ribbon of an order lay across his breast. And there was a diamond cross shining beneath his collar.

"You look magnificent!" Lencia exclaimed.

The Duc smiled and replied,

"And you, my darling Lencia, look exactly as I want you to look."

He kissed her hand and drew her outside to where there was a closed carriage waiting for them.

Behind it was one for Pierre and Alice and they did not say much to each other when they met.

But Lencia knew by the expression on their faces that they were both very much in love with each other.

This completed her happiness.

She would have been extremely worried if she had left Alice alone and unhappy without her.

As they drove off in the carriage, the Duc enthused,

"This, my precious darling, is the most exciting day of my life and we are being married by Cardinal Vaughan, who is the Head of the Roman Catholic Church in England."

"Where are we being married?" Lencia enquired.

"In his private Chapel at the Archbishop's House in Westminster," the Duc answered.

"It sounds very grand," Lencia commented shyly.

"It is," the Duc replied. "The Cardinal has been most understanding and, when I asked for a Priest to marry us, he said that he would be honoured to do it himself."

The Duc gave a little laugh as he added,

"No one can dispute after this that we are completely and properly man and wife, my loved one."

Lencia's fingers tightened on his.

"You are quite certain that you don't want to back out at the last moment?"

The Duc raised her hand and kissed it.

"I will answer that question better tonight," he said. "Now I am only thinking how much I love you and how fortunate I am that I found you after such a long search."

She knew he was thinking of the flowers he had left by the roadside and she said softly,

"I love you with – all my – heart and – my soul, it would be impossible to – love you – more."

"That is what you think now," the Duc replied. "I do promise you, my precious, that our love will increase day by day and night by night."

*

They were married in the very beautiful Chapel, which was filled with white flowers.

The Cardinal was a tall good-looking man and made every word he said seem as though it blessed them.

Pierre acted as best man and Alice was the only other witness.

There were two servers and incense bearers in the Chapel but no one else.

When they knelt at the Altar and the Cardinal blessed them, Lencia felt that she could hear the angels singing overheard.

She was absolutely certain that a bright light then enveloped them that could only have come only from God.

Outside the Chapel the closed carriage was waiting and Lencia kissed Alice and Pierre goodbye.

As she drove off with the Duc, she asked him,

"Where are we going?"

"My yacht is waiting at Westminster Bridge, which is only a very short distance away," he answered.

They reached it in just a few minutes.

Lencia saw at once that it was a large and very impressive-looking modern yacht.

They were piped on board by the crew.

The Captain congratulated them and the Duc told him to move slowly down the Thames towards the sea.

There was luncheon waiting for them in a very attractive Saloon decorated in pale green.

"I never thought of our going away in a yacht," Lencia smiled.

"What could be a better way to escape from the world than to be on the sea where no one can find us?" the Duc asked.

"And where are we going?" Lencia wanted to know.

"To places that you have never seen before and that I want to show you. Also," the Duc added quietly, "to a Heaven all of our own."

Lencia gazed at him and took off her hat.

They ate the delightful food, which she knew had been cooked by a French chef.

It was impossible to think of anything but her husband sitting opposite her at the table.

He was looking at her with an expression in his eyes that told her without words how much he loved her.

When luncheon was finished and they were moving smoothly down river, the Duc said,

"Now we must follow French traditions, which will be very important to us in the future. And there is one which is especially prevalent in France."

"What is it?" Lencia asked him a little nervously.

"A *siesta,* my darling. That is what we both need and what we intend to have."

He took her below and into the Master cabin, which had, of course, been his.

It was filled with more white flowers and their fragrance scented the air.

It was like a bower and she asked with an expression of joy,

"Have you really done all this for me?"

"It is only one of the many things I want to do for you, my precious darling," the Duc answered her. "But I hope you notice that the flowers are like you, white in their purity."

Lencia blushed and he left her to take off his decorations.

She knew what he expected and she undressed quickly.

She slipped into the large bed, which was draped in just the same way as the bed at his Château was draped.

In comparison the cabin was very small, but with all the flowers there was a Fairytale-like feeling about it.

It made Lencia think that everything that was happening was unreal and part of a dream.

'Suppose I should wake up and find that it is all untrue,' she asked herself.

At that moment the Duc came into the cabin.

Impulsively she held out her arms.

"I was afraid – this might be – a dream," she said, "but – you are – here and I am not – dreaming."

"If you are, then I am dreaming too," the Duc countered in a deep voice.

He sat down on the bed looking at her.

"How can you be so beautiful?" he sighed. "So perfect in every way and yet mine."

She put out her hand to touch his, feeling a little thrill as she did so.

"I am so – afraid," she whispered, "that I may – disappoint you."

"That is quite impossible," the Duc insisted. "You are everything I have looked for and thought I would never find. Now you are *mine* and nothing and no one will ever take you from me."

"And you will – teach me to – love you as you – want to be – loved," Lencia asked him shyly.

"You can be quite certain of that," the Duc answered, "and it will be the most exciting thing I have ever done in my whole life."

He climbed into the bed and took her into his arms.

As the shaft of brilliant sunshine she had felt before seemed now to move through her, she knew that this was the perfection of their love.

This was the moment when they would really belong to one another.

The Duc then kissed her, at first gently, as if she was very precious.

She knew in a way that the solemnity of the Marriage Service was still with him as it was with her.

Then his kisses became more possessive.

As his hand touched her, she felt the sunshine which was streaking through her body turn to fire.

She knew that he was feeling the same as he kissed her and went on kissing her.

The flames seemed to rise higher and higher until the ecstasy of them made Lencia feel it was impossible not to die of its wonder.

Then, as the Duc made her his, they were both carried up into the sky.

They touched the sun and held the stars in their arms.

They were in the Heaven that God had made for lovers and which would be theirs for Eternity and beyond.

OTHER BOOKS IN THIS SERIES

The Barbara Cartland Eternal Collection is the unique opportunity to collect all five hundred of the timeless beautiful romantic novels written by the world's most celebrated and enduring romantic author.

Named the Eternal Collection because Barbara's inspiring stories of pure love, just the same as love itself, the books will be published on the internet at the rate of four titles per month until all five hundred are available.

The Eternal Collection, classic pure romance available worldwide for all time.

1. Elizabethan Lover
2. The Little Pretender
3. A Ghost in Monte Carlo
4. A Duel of Hearts
5. The Saint and the Sinner
6. The Penniless Peer
7. The Proud Princess
8. The Dare-Devil Duke
9. Diona and a Dalmatian
10. A Shaft of Sunlight
11. Lies for Love
12. Love and Lucia
13. Love and the Loathsome Leopard
14. Beauty or Brains
15. The Temptation of Torilla
16. The Goddess and the Gaiety Girl
17. Fragrant Flower
18. Look, Listen and Love
19. The Duke and the Preacher's Daughter
20. A Kiss For The King
21. The Mysterious Maid-Servant
22. Lucky Logan Finds Love
23. The Wings of Ecstasy
24. Mission to Monte Carlo
25. Revenge of the Heart
26. The Unbreakable Spell
27. Never Laugh at Love
28. Bride to a Brigand
29. Lucifer and the Angel
30. Journey to a Star
31. Solita and the Spies
32. The Chieftain without a Heart
33. No Escape from Love
34. Dollars for the Duke
35. Pure and Untouched
36. Secrets
37. Fire in the Blood
38. Love, Lies and Marriage
39. The Ghost who fell in love

40. Hungry for Love
41. The wild cry of love
42. The blue eyed witch
43. The Punishment of a Vixen
44. The Secret of the Glen
45. Bride to The King
46. For All Eternity
47. A King in Love
48. A Marriage Made in Heaven
49. Who Can Deny Love?
50. Riding to The Moon
51. Wish for Love
52. Dancing on a Rainbow
53. Gypsy Magic
54. Love in the Clouds
55. Count the Stars
56. White Lilac
57. Too Precious to Lose
58. The Devil Defeated
59. An Angel Runs Away
60. The Duchess Disappeared
61. The Pretty Horse-breakers
62. The Prisoner of Love
63. Ola and the Sea Wolf
64. The Castle made for Love
65. A Heart is Stolen
66. The Love Pirate
67. As Eagles Fly
68. The Magic of Love
69. Love Leaves at Midnight
70. A Witch's Spell
71. Love Comes West
72. The Impetuous Duchess
73. A Tangled Web
74. Love Lifts the Curse
75. Saved By A Saint
76. Love is Dangerous
77. The Poor Governess
78. The Peril and the Prince
79. A Very Unusual Wife
80. Say Yes Samantha
81. Punished with love
82. A Royal Rebuke
83. The Husband Hunters
84. Signpost To Love
85. Love Forbidden
86. Gift of the Gods
87. The Outrageous Lady
88. The Slaves of Love
89. The Disgraceful Duke
90. The Unwanted Wedding
91. Lord Ravenscar's Revenge
92. From Hate to Love
93. A Very Naughty Angel
94. The Innocent Imposter
95. A Rebel Princess
96. A Wish Come True
97. Haunted
98. Passions In The Sand
99. Little White Doves of Love
100. A Portrait of Love
101. The Enchanted Waltz
102. Alone and Afraid
103. The Call of the Highlands
104. The Glittering Lights
105. An Angel in Hell
106. Only a Dream
107. A Nightingale Sang
108. Pride and the Poor Princess
109. Stars in my Heart
110. The Fire of Love
111. A Dream from the Night
112. Sweet Enchantress
113. The Kiss of the Devil
114. Fascination in France
115. Love Runs in
116. Lost Enchantment
117. Love is Innocent
118. The Love Trap
119. No Darkness for Love
120. Kiss from a Stranger
121. The Flame Is Love
122. A Touch Of Love

123. The Dangerous Dandy
124. In Love In Lucca
125. The Karma of Love
126. Magic from the Heart
127. Paradise Found
128. Only Love
129. A Duel with Destiny
130. The Heart of the Clan
131. The Ruthless Rake
132. Revenge Is Sweet
133. Fire on the Snow
134. A Revolution of Love
135. Love at the Helm
136. Listen to Love
137. Love Casts out Fear
138. The Devilish Deception
139. Riding in the Sky
140. The Wonderful Dream
141. This Time it's Love
142. The River of Love
143. A Gentleman in Love
144. The Island of Love
145. Miracle for a Madonna
146. The Storms of Love
147. The Prince and the Pekingese
148. The Golden Cage
149. Theresa and a Tiger
150. The Goddess of Love
151. Alone in Paris
152. The Earl Rings a Belle
153. The Runaway Heart
154. From Hell to Heaven
155. Love in the Ruins
156. Crowned with Love
157. Love is a Maze
158. Hidden by Love
159. Love Is The Key
160. A Miracle In Music
161. The Race For Love
162. Call of The Heart
163. The Curse of the Clan
164. Saved by Love
165. The Tears of Love
166. Winged Magic
167. Born of Love
168. Love Holds the Cards
169. A Chieftain Finds Love
170. The Horizons of Love
171. The Marquis Wins
172. A Duke in Danger
173. Warned by a Ghost
174. Forced to Marry
175. Sweet Adventure
176. Love is a Gamble
177. Love on the Wind
178. Looking for Love
179. Love is the Enemy
180. The Passion and the Flower
181. The Reluctant Bride
182. Safe in Paradise
183. The Temple of Love
184. Love at First Sight
185. The Scots Never Forget
186. The Golden Gondola
187. No Time for Love
188. Love in the Moon
189. A Hazard of Hearts
190. Just Fate
191. The Kiss of Paris
192. Little Tongues of Fire
193. Love under Fire
194. The Magnificent Marriage
195. Moon over Eden
196. The Dream and The Glory
197. A Victory for Love
198. A Princess in Distress
199. A Gamble with Hearts
200. Love strikes a Devil
201. In the arms of Love
202. Love in the Dark
203. Love Wins
204. The Marquis Who Hated Women
205. Love is Invincible
206. Love Climbs in